"One night. I'll reduce the bet to one night."

Slowly she turned to face him, her expression haughty and scornful. "Pity, Rico? From you? I'm surprised. But I must refuse your gallant gesture. A bet is a bet. You demanded I be your mistress for a month, so your mistress for a month I will be. Not a day less. Not a day more."

Her contrariness jolted him. Was this her pride still talking, or did she have some other secret agenda? Whatever the case, experience had taught Rico never to try to second-guess Renée, so he just shrugged.

"Fine by me." Far be it from him to lessen her sentence. She'd made her bed now. Let her lie in it.

"You might think that tonight," she replied. "You might think differently in a month's time."

"Is that a threat, Renée? Or a challenge?"

"It's a promise"

Three Rich Men

*Three Australian billionaires;
they can have anything and anyone...
except three beautiful women...*

Meet Charles, Rico and Ali,
three incredibly wealthy friends all living in
Sydney. They meet every Friday night to play
poker and exchange news about business and
their pleasures—which include the pursuit of
Sydney's most beautiful women.

Up until now, no single woman has ever
managed to pin down the elusive, exclusive and
eminently eligible bachelors. But that's all about
to change.... But will these three rich men marry
for love—or are they desired for their money?

A Rich Man's Revenge—Charles's story
#2349 October 2003

Mistress for a Month—Rico's story
#2361 December 2003

Sold to the Sheikh—Ali's story
#2374 February 2004

Available only from Harlequin Presents®.

Miranda Lee

MISTRESS FOR A MONTH

Three Rich Men

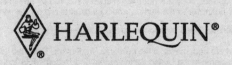

HARLEQUIN®

TORONTO • NEW YORK • LONDON
AMSTERDAM • PARIS • SYDNEY • HAMBURG
STOCKHOLM • ATHENS • TOKYO • MILAN • MADRID
PRAGUE • WARSAW • BUDAPEST • AUCKLAND

ISBN 0-373-12361-2

MISTRESS FOR A MONTH

First North American Publication 2003.

Visit us at www.eHarlequin.com

Printed in U.S.A.

CHAPTER ONE

RICO MANDRETTI jumped into his shiny red Ferrari and headed, not towards Randwick Racecourse, but straight for his parents' place on the rural outskirts of Sydney. His plans had changed. Last night had changed them.

'Not today,' Rico muttered to himself as he sped out through Sydney's sprawling western suburbs, oblivious of the second glances he received from most of the women in the cars he passed, and *all* of the women in the cars he was forced to idle next to when the lights turned red.

Only one woman occupied Rico's mind these days. Only one woman did he crave to look at him as if he was a man worth looking at and not some prima-donna playboy with no substance at all.

For over five years he'd endured Renée Selinsky's barbs over the card table every Friday night, as well as at the races on a Saturday afternoon.

Five years was a long time to tolerate such treatment. *Too* long.

Yet he had to confess that till last night he'd enjoyed their verbal sparring in a perverse fashion, despite the fact Renée usually got the better of him. When she'd temporarily subjected him to the cold-shoulder treatment a few months back, he'd hated it. Rico discovered during that difficult time that he'd rather have his buttons pressed than be ignored.

Still, Renée had pressed his buttons one too many times last night.

Be damned if he was going to be on the end of that woman's caustic tongue again today at the races. Enough was enough!

The lights turned green and he floored the accelerator. The Ferrari leapt forward, tyres screeching slightly as he scorched up the road. But, given the speed limit on that section of highway, and the regular traffic lights, there was no solace for Rico's frustration in speeding, and no escape for his thoughts.

Soon he was idling at the next set of red lights, practically grinding his teeth when his mind returned once more to his nemesis.

She'd be at the races by now, probably sitting at the bar in the members' stand, sipping a glass of champagne and looking her usual cool and classy self, not caring a whit that he hadn't turned up, whilst he was sitting here in his car, stewing away, already regretting his decision not to go. He *loved* the races. They were one of his passions in life. And one of hers, unfortunately.

That was how he'd met Renée in the first place, through their mutual love of horse racing. Just over five years ago she'd become the third partner in the syndicate he and his best friend, Charles, had formed with the help of Ward Jackman, one of Sydney's up-and-coming young horse trainers.

Rico could still remember the first day he met the up-till-then mysterious Mrs Selinsky. The three co-owners had gathered at Randwick races to see their first horse race, a lovely chestnut filly named Flame of Gold.

Before that day, Rico had only known of his lady

co-owner's existence on paper. He'd no idea that she was also Renée, the owner of *Renée's* modeling agency and the widow of Joseph Selinsky, a very wealthy banker who'd been almost forty years his second wife's senior, and who'd passed away the previous year. He *did* know she was a rich widow, but he'd pictured an overweight, over-groomed madam in her sixties or seventies with more money than she could spend in the beauty salon, and a penchant for gambling.

Nothing had prepared Rico for the sleekly sophisticated, super-stylish and super-intelligent thirty-year-old which Mrs Selinsky had proved to be. And certainly nothing had prepared Rico for her instantly negative reaction to him. He was used to being fawned over by the opposite sex, not the exact opposite.

Looking back, he'd been attracted to her right from first sight, despite his having another woman on his arm that day. His fiancée, in fact. Jasmine. The bright, bubbly, beautifully blonde Jasmine. He'd thought himself in love with Jasmine, and he'd married her a month later.

It was a marriage which had been doomed from the start. God, if he'd only known then what he knew now.

But would that have changed anything? he pondered as he revved up the Ferrari's engine in anticipation of these lights turning green. What if he'd realised Jasmine was an unfeeling fortune-hunter before their wedding? Or that his so-called love for her was the result of his being cleverly conned and constantly flattered? What if he'd broken up with his faking fiancée and pursued the enigmatic and striking Renée instead?

Renée's reaction to him might have been very different if he'd been single and available five years ago, instead of engaged and supposedly besotted with his fiancée.

After all, he was Rico Mandretti, the producer and star of *A Passion for Pasta*, the most successful cooking show on television. The merry widow—as he'd soon nicknamed Renée—obviously knew the value of a dollar, given she'd already married once for money. Rico could not imagine a woman of her youth and beauty marrying a man in his sixties for *love*.

Whilst Rico hadn't had as many dollars in the bank as Renée's late husband at that stage, he'd still been well-heeled, with the potential for earning more in the years to come, which had since proven correct. His little cooking show—as Renée mockingly liked to call it—was now syndicated to over twenty countries and the money was rolling in, with more business ventures popping up each year, from cookbooks to product endorsements to his more recent idea of franchising *A Passion for Pasta* restaurants in every major city in Australia.

Aside from his earning potential, he'd also only been twenty-nine back then, brimming with macho confidence and testosterone. In his sexual prime, so to speak.

Rico liked to think Renée would have fallen into his arms, but he knew he was just kidding himself. He'd been split up from Jasmine for two years now, his divorce signed and sealed over a year ago, and Renée's negative attitude to him hadn't changed one bit. If anything, she'd grown more hostile to him whilst his desire for her had become unbearably acute.

It pained Rico to think that she found nothing attractive in him whatsoever. In fact, she obviously despised him. Why? What had he ever done to her to cause such antagonism? Was it his Italian background? She sometimes sounded off about his being a Latin-lover type, all hormones and no brains.

Rico knew there was more to himself than that. But not when he was around her these days, he accepted ruefully. Lately, whenever she turned those slanting green eyes on him and made one of her biting comments, *he* turned into the kind of mindless macho animal she obviously thought him. His ability to play poker suffered. Hell, his ability to do anything well suffered! The charm he was famous for disappeared, along with his capacity to think.

Aah, but he could still *feel*. Even as his blood boiled with the blackest of resentments, his body would burn with a white-hot need. That was why he was avoiding his nemesis this weekend. Because Rico suspected he was nearing spontaneous combustion where she was concerned. Who knew what he would do or say the next time she goaded him the way she had last night?

'Now, if you'd married someone like Dominique, Rico,' Renée had remarked after Charles announced his wife was expecting, 'you'd have a baby or two of your own by now. If you're really as keen on the idea of a traditional marriage and family as you claim, then for pity's sake stop dilly-dallying with the Leannes of this world and find yourself a nice girl who'll give you what you supposedly want.'

Rico had literally had to bite his tongue to stop

himself from retorting that he took women like Leanne to bed in a vain attempt to burn out the frustration he experienced from not being able to have *her*.

Somehow, he'd managed an enigmatic little smile, and experienced some satisfaction in seeing her green eyes darken with a frustration of her own.

Mark one up for Rico for a change!

But for how long could he manage such iron self-control? Not too much longer, he suspected.

Charles and Ali wouldn't know what hit them if and when he exploded. Rico might have been born and brought up here in Sydney, but he was Italian through and through, with an Italian's volatile temperament.

A peasant, Renée had once labelled him. Which was quite true. He did come from peasant stock. And was proud of it!

Rico's other two Friday-night poker-playing partners were blue-blood gentlemen by comparison. His best friend, Charles, was Charles Brandon, a few years older than Rico and the owner of Brandon Beer, Australia's premier boutique brewery. Ali was Prince Ali of Dubar, the youngest son of an oil-rich sheikh, dispatched to Australia a decade before to run the royal Arab family's thoroughbred interests down under.

Both men had been born into money, but neither was anything like the lazy, spoilt, silver-spoon variety of human being whom Rico despised.

Charles had spent years dragging his family firm back from the brink of bankruptcy after his profligate father died, leaving Brandon Beer in a right old mess.

That achievement had taken grit, determination and vision, all qualities Rico admired.

Ali didn't act like some pampered prince, either. He worked very hard, running the thoroughbred stud which occupied over a thousand acres of prime horse land in the Hunter Valley. Rico had seen with his own eyes how hands-on Ali was with running and managing that complex and extremely large establishment.

It had been Ali, actually, who'd brought the four poker-players together. He was the breeder of Flame of Gold. After she'd won the Silver Slipper Stakes, the three ecstatic owners and one highly elated breeder had had a celebratory dinner together. Over a seafood banquet down at the quay, they'd discovered a mutual love, not just of racehorses but also of playing cards. Gambling of various kinds, it seemed, was in all their blood. They'd played their first game of poker together later that night and made a pact to play together every Friday night after that.

Being ill or overseas were the only excuses not to show up at the presidential suite at Sydney's five-star Regency Hotel every Friday night at eight. That was where Ali stayed each weekend, flying in from his country property by helicopter late on a Friday and returning on the Sunday.

Rico smiled wryly when he thought of how, when he'd been hospitalised with an injured knee after a skiing mishap last year, he'd insisted that the others come to his hospital room for their Friday-night poker session. The evening had not been a great success, however, with Ali having a couple of security guards trailing along.

Looking back, he could see that his own insistence

on playing that night, despite his handicapped condition, highlighted his rapidly growing obsession with the merry widow. He hadn't been able to stand the thought of not seeing her that week. Now he wasn't sure if he could stand seeing her again at all! He was fast reaching breaking point. Something was going to give. And soon.

Rico's stress level lessened slightly once the more densely populated suburbs were behind him and his eyes could feast on more grass and trees. He breathed in deeply through his nostrils, smelling the cleaner air and smiling with fond memories as the city was finally left behind and he drove past familiar places. The small bush primary school he'd attended as a child. The creek where he'd gone swimming in the summer. The old community hall where he'd taken dancing lessons, much to his father's disgust.

As far back as he could remember, Rico had been determined to one day be a star. By the time he turned twelve, he'd envisaged a career on the stage in the sort of singing, dancing, foot-stomping show he adored. But whilst his dancing technique was excellent, he'd grown too tall and too big to look as elegant and graceful as shorter, leaner dancers. On top of that, his singing left a lot to be desired. Once that career path was dashed, he'd focused his ambition on straight acting, seeing himself as an Australian John Travolta. People often said he looked like him.

His early acting career had been a hit-and-miss affair, especially after he'd failed to get into any of the élite and very restricted Australian acting academies. He did succeed in landing a few bit parts in soaps, plus a couple of television advertisements and one minor role in a TV movie, but at a lot of auditions he was told he was too big, and too Italian-looking.

Although not entirely convinced, Rico finally began looking more at a career behind the camera rather than in front of it. Producing and directing became his revised ambition, both on television and in the booming Australian film industry. He learned the ropes as a camera and sound man, working for Fortune productions, who were responsible for the most popular shows on TV back then. He watched and observed and learned till he decided he was ready to make his own show.

With backing from his large family—Rico had three indulgent older brothers and five doting older sisters—he started production on *A Passion for Pasta*, having noted that cooking and lifestyle programmes were really taking off. But the Australian-Italian chef he hired for the pilot episode turned out to be a bundle of nerves in front of the camera, with Rico constantly having to jump in and show him what to do, and how to do it.

Despite his not having any formal training as a chef, it soon became obvious that he was a natural in the part as the show's host. Rico had finally found his niche. Suddenly, his size didn't matter, his Italian looks were an asset and the Italian accent he could bung on without any trouble at all gave a touch of authenticity. It also helped that he really was a very good amateur cook, his mother having taught him. It was Signora Mandretti's very real passion for pasta, and her creativeness with the product—feeding her large family on a tight budget required more than a little inventiveness—which had inspired the show's title and content.

A Passion for Pasta was an instant success once Rico had found a buyer, and he hadn't looked back.

Not that any of his successes ever impressed Renée. They had certainly impressed Jasmine, however. She'd known a good thing when she saw it.

Rico pulled a face at the memory of the gold-digger he'd married. He was still flabbergasted over how much the family law court judge had awarded her for the privilege of being a pampered princess for three years.

Still, it had been worth any price in the end to get Jasmine out of his life, although he'd deeply resented her demanding—and *getting*, mind you—both their Bondi Beach apartment *and* his favourite car, a one-off black Porsche which he'd had especially fitted out with black leather seats and thick black carpet on the floors.

Black had always been Rico's favourite colour, both in clothes and cars. He'd bought the red Ferrari he was now driving on a mad impulse, telling himself that a change was as good as a holiday, an act which had rebounded on him when Renée had recently seen him getting into it in the car park at the races.

'I should have known that the red Ferrari was your car,' she'd said with a sniff of her delicately flaring nostrils. 'What else would an Italian playboy drive?'

On that occasion—as was depressingly often the case these days—he hadn't been able to think of a snappy comeback quick enough, and she'd driven off in her sedate and stylish BMW with a superior smirk on her face.

His mind returning to Renée once more brought a scowl to his. He'd promised himself earlier he wasn't going to think about that witch today. He'd already given her enough thought to last a lifetime!

The sight of a very familiar roadside postbox coming up on his right soon wiped the scowl from his face.

His parents' property wasn't anything fancy. Just a few acres of market garden with a large but plain two-storeyed cream brick house perched on the small rise in the middle of the land. But Rico's heart seemed to expand at the sight of it and he found himself smiling as he turned into the driveway.

There was nothing like coming home. Home to your roots, and to people who really knew you, and loved you all the same.

CHAPTER TWO

TERESA MANDRETTI was picking some herbs from her private vegetable and herb garden—the one *she* planted and personally tended—when a figure moved into the corner of her eye.

'Enrico!' she exclaimed on lifting her head and seeing her youngest child walking towards her. 'You startled me. I wasn't expecting you till tomorrow.'

The first Sunday of the month was traditionally family day at the Mandretti household, with her youngest son always coming home to share lunch with his parents, plus as many of his siblings and their families that could make it.

'Mum.' He opened his arms and drew her into a wrap-around hug, his six-foot-two, broad-shouldered frame totally enveloping her own short, plump one.

How he had come to be so big and tall, Teresa could only guess. His father, Frederico, was not a big man. When the family back in Italy had seen photos of Enrico at his twenty-first birthday, they said he had to be a throwback to Frederico's father, who'd reputedly been a giant of a man. Teresa had never actually met her father-in-law. Frederico Senior had been killed in a fight with another man when he was only thirty-five, having flown into a jealous rage when this other fellow had paid what he called ''improper'' attention to his wife.

Teresa could well imagine that this was where

Enrico got quite a few of his genes. Her youngest son had a temper on him, too.

'Have you had lunch?' she asked when her son finally let her come up for air. He was a hugger, was Enrico, like all the Mandrettis. Teresa was from more reserved stock. Which was why she'd found Frederico Mandretti so attractive. He'd taken no notice of her shyness and swept her off to his bed before she could say no. They'd been married a few weeks later with her first son already in her belly. They'd migrated to Australia a few months after that, just in time for Frederico the Third to be born in their new country.

'No, but I'm not hungry,' came her son's surprising reply.

Teresa's eyes narrowed. Not *hungry*? Her *Enrico*, who could eat a horse even if he was dying! Something was not right here.

'What's wrong, Enrico?' she asked with a mother's worried eyes and voice.

'Nothing's wrong, Mum. Truly. I had a very large, very late breakfast, that's all. Where's Dad?'

'He's gone to the races. Not the horse races. The dog races. Down at Appin. Uncle Guiseppe has a couple of runners today.'

'Dad should buy himself a greyhound or two. The walking would do him good. Get rid of that spare tyre he's carrying around his middle. I think he's been eating too much of your pasta.'

Teresa bridled. 'Are you saying your *papa* is fat?'

'Not fat, exactly. Just well fed.'

Teresa suspected Enrico was deliberately diverting the subject away from himself. She knew all her children well, but she knew Enrico even better than the others. He'd come along when she'd thought there

would be no more *bambinos*. She'd already had eight
children, one each year or so, three boys followed by
five girls. After giving birth to Katrina, the doctor had
told her she should not have any more babies. Her
body was exhausted. So she'd gone on the Pill with
her sensible priest's permission, and for the next nine
years, had not had the worry of being pregnant.

But the Pill was not perfect, it seemed, and another
child had eventually been conceived. Although she
was worried, a termination had not even been consid-
ered, and fortunately Teresa had been blessed with a
trouble-free pregnancy that time and an amazingly
easy birth. Enrico being a boy was an added bonus
after having had five girls in a row.

Of course, he'd been very spoiled, by *all* of them,
but especially his sisters. Still, despite the temper tan-
trums he threw when he didn't get what he wanted,
Enrico had been a loving child who had grown into
a loving man. Everyone in the family adored him, not
the least being herself. Teresa would never have admitted it openly, but Enrico held a special place in
her heart, possibly because he was her youngest. With
the ten-year age gap between Enrico and his closest
sister, Teresa had been able to devote a lot of time to
raising her last baby. Enrico had followed her around
like a little puppy, and mother and son were very
close.

Enrico could *never* fool her. Aside from his sus-
picious lack of hunger today, she knew something had
to be up to take him away from the races on a
Saturday afternoon. With a mother's intuition, she
sensed it had something to do with a woman. Possibly
with that Renée lady he often spoke about but whom
she'd never met, the one he played poker with every

Friday night and who was part of his racing syndicate. Teresa had sensed an odd note in his voice whenever he mentioned her.

And he mentioned her quite a bit.

Teresa would have liked to ask him about her but suspected that the direct approach would be a waste of time. At thirty-four, her youngest son was long past the age that he confided matters concerning his personal and private life to his mother. Which was a pity. If he'd consulted her before he'd become tangled up with that Jasmine creature, she could have saved her son a lot of heartache.

Now, *there* was a nasty piece of work if ever there was one. Clever, though. Butter wouldn't have melted in her mouth around the Mandrettis till the wedding, after which she'd gradually stopped coming to family functions, making poorer and poorer excuses till there weren't any left to be made.

Fortunately, she was now past history. Though not generally believing in divorce, Teresa was a realist. Some divorces were like taking the Pill. A necessity. Still, Teresa didn't want Enrico repeating his mistake by getting tangled up with another unsuitable woman.

'Did you play cards last night?' she asked as she bent to pull a few sprigs of mint.

'Of course,' came her son's less than enlightening reply.

'Charles well, is he?' Charles was the only one of Enrico's three poker-playing friends whom Teresa had actually met, despite her having invited the trio to several parties over the years. That Renée woman was a bit like Jasmine, always having some excuse not to come. The other man, the Arab sheikh, had also always declined, though his refusals Teresa understood.

Enrico had explained that Prince Ali kept very much to himself, because of his huge wealth and family connections. Apparently, the poor man could never go anywhere in public without having a bodyguard accompany him. Sometimes *two*.

What a terrible way to live!

Enrico had to cope with a degree of harassment from the Press and photographers himself, but he could still come and go as he pleased without feeling he was in any physical danger.

'Charles is very well,' her son answered. 'He and his wife are going to have a baby. In about six months time, I gather.'

'How lovely for them,' Teresa enthused as she straightened, all the while wondering if that was what had upset Enrico. He'd always wanted children of his own. Most Italian men did. It was part of their culture, to father sons to proudly carry on their name, and daughters to dote upon.

Teresa had no doubt Enrico would make a wonderful father. He was marvellous with all his nephews and nieces. It pained Teresa sometimes to see how they always gravitated towards their uncle Rico, who was never too busy to play with them. He should be playing with children of his own.

If only she could *say* so.

Teresa suddenly decided that she was too old and too Italian for the tactful, indirect approach.

'When are you going to stop being silly and get married again, Enrico?'

He laughed. 'Please don't hold back, Mum. Say it like you see it.'

'I do not mean any disrespect, Enrico, but someone has to say something. You're thirty-four years old and not getting any younger. You need a wife, one who will be more than happy to stay home and have your children. A man of your looks and success should have no trouble finding a suitable young lady. If you like, we could ask the family at home to look around for a nice Italian girl.'

That should spur him on to do the looking around for himself! Enrico might have Italian blood flowing in his veins but he was very Australian in many ways. Look at the way he always called her *Mum* and his father Dad, whereas his older brothers and sisters always called them Mama and Papa.

Naturally, arranged marriages were anathema to her youngest son. He believed in marrying for love, and, up to a point, so did Teresa.

But best not to tell him that.

Her son's look of horror was very satisfying.

'Don't start that old-fashioned nonsense, Mum. When and if I marry again, it will be to a lady of my choosing. And it will be for love.'

'That's what you said the first time, and look where it got you!'

'Hopefully, not every woman is like Jasmine.'

'I still can't understand what you saw in that girl.'

He laughed. 'That's because you're not a man.'

Teresa shook her head at her son. Did he think she was so old that she had no memory of sex? She was only seventy-three, not a hundred and three.

'She might have had a pretty face and a good body but she was vain and selfish,' Teresa pronounced firmly. 'You'd have to be a fool not to see that.'

'Men in love *are* fools, Mum,' he retorted with a

self-mocking edge which Teresa immediately picked
up on.

She stared up at Enrico but he wasn't looking at
her. He was off in another world. It came to her that
he wasn't thinking of Jasmine, but some other
woman. Teresa's heart lurched at the realisation that
her youngest son, the apple of her eye, was in love
with a *new* woman.

Dear God, she hoped and prayed that it *wasn't* his
card-playing friend. Despite never having met the
lady, Teresa had gleaned quite a few facts about her
from Enrico's various comments. She was a widow
for starters, a wealthy widow, whose late husband had
been a much older man. An ex-model, she was also
a highly astute businesswoman who ran a modelling
agency in the city. To cap it all off, she was in her
mid-thirties and had never had any children. Probably
hadn't wanted any. A lot of career women didn't.

In other words, she was not good daughter-in-law
material for Teresa Mandretti.

'I won't be coming home for lunch tomorrow,
Mum,' Enrico said abruptly. 'I have somewhere else
I have to go.'

'Where?'

'The man who trains our horses is having a special
open day at his place for all his owners to celebrate
the arrival of spring, and presumably get everyone in
the right mood for the imminent spring racing carni-
vals.'

'Like a party,' his mother said.

'Yes. I suppose you could call it that,' Rico agreed.

Earlier this year, Ward's very savvy personal as-
sistant, a smart little piece called Lisa, had instigated
the increasingly popular tradition amongst horse train-

ers of having an open day for the owners every Sunday where they could visit their horses, discuss their valuable charges' prospects with the trainer or his stable foreman, then enjoy each other's company afterwards over a buffet lunch. But tomorrow was going to be extra-special, with the best of champagne and food.

Rico hadn't been going to attend, the same way he never attended any open day which fell on the first Sunday of the month, because it clashed with his monthly family get-together, an occasion which was far more important to him than socialising with the rich and famous, or having another clash with Renée.

But tomorrow was different. Tomorrow was D day. Desperation day.

'I see,' his mother said thoughtfully. 'Will Charles be there?'

'Probably not. He's not as interested in the horses as he once was.'

'That is understandable, Enrico. He has more to think about now that he has a wife and a little *bambino* on the way. What about your sheikh friend? *He's* not married. Will he be there?'

'No. You know Ali rarely goes to functions like that.'

Which left...the widow, Teresa deduced. Unless this horse trainer had a blonde girl jockey in his employ.

Enrico was partial to blondes. But tall, curvy ones, come to think of it, not teenie-weenie skinny ones. Which begged the question of what this Renée looked like.

She had to be tall, since she was an ex-model. And probably blonde, since her son was attracted. Maybe even busty, as Jasmine had been. Gone were the days when models had to be flat-chested.

'What about your other card-playing friend?' Teresa couldn't resist asking. 'The lady. Renée, isn't it? Will she be there?'

He smiled. He actually smiled. But it wasn't a happy smile. More a wryly resigned one.

'Oh, yes. Sure to be.'

Which gave Teresa the answer she was looking for. Enrico *was* in love with this Renée, but the lady didn't return his feelings.

Now Teresa didn't know what to think, or to feel. That any woman could resist her Enrico annoyed her considerably. Her youngest son was irresistible, in her opinion. At the same time, the last woman she would want him getting tangled up with was another creature like that gold-digging Jasmine.

So perhaps it was just as well this Renée didn't fancy him. But truly, she had to be some kind of blind fool. Enrico was a magnificent man. A man amongst men. What kind of stupid woman would not want him in her bed, and in her heart?

Teresa dropped the sprigs of mint she'd picked into the front pocket of her apron and linked arms with her handsome son. 'Come, Enrico. I have another pasta recipe to show you. A brand-new one.' And she drew him towards the back door, chattering away all the while, showering him with her love and approval.

Rico allowed himself to be cosseted and comforted, because he knew that, come tomorrow, he would be going into battle again with his nemesis. His decision just now to attend the open day showed how addicted he was to that witch's company. He simply could not go a single weekend without seeing her. Avoiding her at the races this afternoon hadn't worked at all.

It was a deplorable state of affairs. But what could he do about it? How could he change it? How could he change *her*?

He couldn't. All he could do was change himself. But how, was the problem. How did you stop yourself craving what you'd become addicted to?

He'd tried the out-of-sight, out-of-mind method, and that hadn't worked. Going cold turkey didn't apply, as he hadn't yet had the pleasure of having what he craved. There was counselling, he supposed, but he just couldn't picture that working, either.

So tell me, Mr Mandretti, what is it about this lady that you like so much?

Let's see, now, Doc, he could hear himself replying. *First there are her eyes. The slanting green ones which gleam with contempt every time they look at me. And then there's her gorgeous mouth, which cuts me to ribbons every time she opens it. But mostly there's her long, tall, far-too-slender body, which I shouldn't find incredibly sexy but I do!*

He'd be diagnosed a masochist with obsessional compulsive disorder and sent home with a swag of antidepressants, an appointment for a therapy session every week into eternity and a bill you couldn't climb over.

No, he wasn't going to try counselling.

Which left what?

The answer really was quite simple...if you were prepared to embrace the joys of rejection. He could ask the merry widow out. On a date.

He had asked her out before, of course. Many

times. But under the guise of a general invitation to one of his mother's parties.

Renée had always refused. Oh, she'd been polite enough on those occasions, but the bottom line was always the same. Clearly, she didn't want to spend any more time in his company than that which she presently endured.

To ask her out on a one-on-one basis was true masochism. But damn it all, what did he have to lose?

Tomorrow, he would jump right into the lion pit and put his head in the lioness's mouth. What happened after that was anybody's guess.

CHAPTER THREE

AROUND twelve-thirty the following day, a gut-tightened Rico left his new penthouse apartment—the one he'd snapped up from Charles when he relocated to the North Shore—and rode his private elevator down to the basement car park. There he strode quickly over to his Ferrari, jumped in behind the wheel, shoved in the key and started the engine.

He was running a bit late, considering the invitation stated from eleven onwards, but it wouldn't take him long to get there. Fifteen minutes at most. That was one of the great things about Charles' old place, aside from the views. Its location down near Circular Quay was so darned convenient.

Rico hadn't exited the underground car park and driven more than a block before realising that having the top down on his car was downright uncomfortable. The day was not a picture-perfect spring day, unlike yesterday, which had been lovely and warm.

As he grudgingly zapped the top up on his car, Rico told himself that the grey skies were not an omen of the day ahead, just typical of Sydney in early September. He still marvelled how the Sydney Olympics—which had been held in that same month—had been blessed with such consistently magnificent weather. Most of the time you never knew what you were going to get in spring in Sydney till you stuck your head out of the window in the morning. Relying on the weather forecast the night before was as silly as thinking Renée was actually going to say yes to his asking her out today.

Rico still could not believe he was actually doing this. Talk about masochistic!

But all the self-lectures in the world were not going to change his mind. Rico had always believed in going after what he wanted, at least till it was irrevocably certain that he could not have what he wanted, such as a career on the stage. Then and only then did he move on from such a goal, putting his energies into something more attainable.

So till Renée looked him straight in the face and said *no way, José* to going out with him, Rico harboured some small hope that he might succeed in his mission improbable. He even managed to convince himself during the brief drive over to Randwick that he had a reasonable chance of success.

After all, the merry widow had no permanent partner. If she had, such a partner would surely have accompanied her to the races sometimes. Yet she always came alone. Added to that was the interesting fact that, except on the rare occasion she'd gone overseas on a business trip, she *always* showed up to play poker on a Friday night. What woman involved with, or living with, some man would be so consistent?

Not that Rico imagined for one moment Renée was leading a nun-like lifestyle. She had to have had men friends since becoming a widow. Lovers, in other words. It had been over five years after all, far too long a time for a woman like her to have spent every night alone.

For some reason—possibly self-protection—Rico hadn't given much thought in the past to whom Renée actually slept with. Suddenly, this subject was the sole focus of his brain. After discarding all sorts of scenarios from secret affairs with married men to one-night stands with commitment-phobic divorcees, he decided she probably enjoyed strictly sexual flings with the toy-boy variety, selected from the huge stable of young male models who were contracted to her modelling agency.

Rico could easily see Renée in that kind of relationship. She would always want to be the boss, to always be on top.

The thought of her being on top of *him* did things to his body which hadn't been done so swiftly or so savagely since he was a teenager. He winced then tried to rearrange the bulge in his trousers to ease his discomfort, but it was a lost cause. Nothing was going to solve his problem, nothing except full body contact with Renée.

As Rico turned into the Randwick street where Ward's home and stables were located, he vowed to succeed in making Renée go out with him—*and* go to bed with him—even if he had to sell his soul to the devil to do so!

The sight of her blue BMW parked at the kerb right outside Ward's front gate gave Rico's black resolve a momentary jolt. She was there, waiting for him to make a fool of himself. No escape now, not unless he wimped out. And Rico was no wimp.

For a split-second the car-lined street almost gave him an excuse to drive on, to forget this insane mission. But then a gap presented itself in between a silver Jag and a dark blue Merc. Ward's owners were not short of a dollar. With a resigned sigh, Rico expertly angled his Ferrari into the rather tight spot and cut off the engine.

After a glance at his watch—it was getting on for one—he dragged himself out from behind the wheel, slammed the door and zapped the immobiliser. Almost as an afterthought, he checked his appearance in the side-mirror, finger-combing his messy hair back from his face before frowning at the dark stubble on his cheeks and chin. He never shaved on the weekend—something Renée had no doubt noticed in the past—so he hadn't wanted it to seem as if he'd been sprucing himself up specially for her.

Still, given he was planning to ask her out—view full sex at the end of the night—this now seemed a stupid train of thought. Totally…utterly…stupid! Which meant he was running true to form. Once Renée came into the equation in anything he did, off went his head and on went a pumpkin.

But faint heart never won fat turkey, Rico reminded himself doggedly. Or the hand of the fair lady. Not that he wanted to marry the merry widow. He wasn't *that* crazy! All he wanted was a few nights in her bed, after which he was sure that this perverse sexual obsession he'd been suffering from these past five years would burn itself out.

He didn't love her. Lord, no. No way! What was there to love? She was no better than Jasmine, really. Just another hard-nosed, hard-hearted, mercenary madam who specialised in making fools of men, namely him.

With that charming thought in mind, Rico slid his hands into the pockets of his black trousers and walked somewhat reluctantly back up the street to Ward's establishment, throwing Renée's BMW a testy look as he passed by. She must have been the first guest to arrive to get such a prize spot.

Rico stood for a moment at Ward's front gate, staring blankly up at the trainer's very stylish two-storey home and trying to get his brain into gear. All the owners would have finished visiting their horses by now. They'd all be inside, tucking into the champers and caviare. All except...Renée.

More than likely she'd still be at the stables, fussing over their syndicate's most expensive purchase to date, a three-year-old black colt which they'd bought from Ali as a yearling but which had gone seriously shin-sore during his first preparation and been turned out to mature. He'd been back in training for a few weeks, and Ward's PA had told Rico on the phone the other night—the notoriously taciturn trainer rarely spoke to owners in person over the phone—that Ebony Fire had come back a treat and was working the place down. No doubt Lisa had relayed the same news to Renée.

Although Rico knew surprisingly little about Renée on a personal basis, he knew how she felt about the horses she owned and part-owned. She loved them. Loved being around them. Loved touching them and talking to them. On the couple of occasions that he *had* come to an open Sunday prior to today, Renée had been difficult to pry away from the stables.

'I don't come here to eat,' she'd snapped at him once when he'd suggested going inside for lunch. 'I come here to visit with my horses.'

Rico smiled wryly at the memory. Oh, yes. She would not have gone inside yet. He was sure of it.

Which was a comfort. The prospect of propositioning the object of his desire in privacy was infinitely preferable to doing so in a roomful of people where others might hear her hysterical laughter. This way, he could keep his humiliation to himself.

Scooping in a deep and hopefully calming breath, he spun on his heels and headed for the side-path, which bypassed Ward's house and led round to where the stables were located at the rear of the property. At the end of this path was a gate which was always manned by a security guard. Today's man was called Jed, a big, beefy fellow who knew all of Ward's owners by sight.

'Afternoon, Mr Mandretti,' Jed said as he opened the gate to let Rico in. 'You're running a bit late. All the others have gone in to lunch.'

Rico's heart sank, till he realised Jed couldn't possibly know that for a fact from where he was stationed. Ward's stable complex was shaped in a square with an internal courtyard. Each side of the square housed six stalls along with feed and tack rooms at the ends of the rows, with staff quarters on the floor above.

Whilst Jed could peer through the gap at the nearest corner into the courtyard beyond, he couldn't possibly see inside the stalls, which was where Renée always ventured. It was never enough for her to stroke her horses' heads over the stall doors. If the horse was docile enough, she would be right in there, up close and personal.

'No worries, Jed,' Rico replied as he walked on in. 'I haven't come to eat today. See you.'

The courtyard was deserted except for one stable-hand, who was hosing away the last of the horsy deposits from the pavings, legacies of their having been walked around on show for their owners.

'Working hard there, Neil, I see,' Rico said as he approached.

The young lad glanced up with surprise and pleasure on his face.

'Why, hello there, Mr Mandretti,' Neil replied, swiftly turning off the hose so that their esteemed visitor could pass by without getting anything splattered on his very smart and expensive-looking black clothes. If there was one owner Neil liked almost as much as he liked Mrs Selinsky, it was Mr Mandretti. For one thing, he always remembered his name, not like a lot of the *hoi polloi*. You'd never know he was a famous TV star by the way he acted. He was so nice and friendly. Of course, no one was as nice as Mrs Selinsky. Now there was one genuine lady. Generous, too. Every time one of her horses won any prize money, she gave all the grooms a bonus.

But it wasn't just her handing out cash which made everyone here warm to her. It was the way she was with the horses. She really cared about them. Even the boss liked Mrs Selinsky. You could tell because he actually talked to her. And the boss was not one for idle chit-chat.

'You'll be here to see your colt, I suppose,' Neil said. 'Mrs Selinsky's still in there with him. I think she'd sleep in that stall if the boss'd let her.'

Rico decided then and there that if there was such a thing as reincarnation he wanted to come back as one of Renée's racehorses.

'What stall is Blackie in?' Rico asked. Blackie was Ebony Fire's stable name.

'Number eighteen. The last on that row over there. I know it's not for me to say, but if he runs as good

as he looks this time in, you'll have a class-one winner there for sure.'

'Let's hope so, Neil. But there's many a slip twixt
the training track and the winner's circle.'

'Aye. That there is. But then that's the way of the
racin' game, isn't it? It's all a gamble. A bit like life.'

Rico nodded. Neil was right. Life *was* a gamble.
Sometimes you won and sometimes you lost.
Knowledge, however, increased your odds of winning. Suddenly, he wished he knew a lot more about
Mrs Renée Selinsky. But it was too late to worry
about that now. The time had come to take his
chances. To gamble on winning the Maiden Stakes.
Trouble was, he was a long shot and long shots didn't
win too often.

Despite his growing inner tension, he waved a
jaunty goodbye to Neil before making his way
straight for stall number eighteen.

Several of the horses whose heads were hanging
over the doors whinnied to him as he strode past.
Ebony Fire, however, was not one of them. At first
glance, stall number eighteen seemed empty. But,
once Rico's eyes adjusted to the dimmer light inside,
he saw that the black colt was standing on a thick
bed of straw in the far corner, having his flank stroked
and being talked as if he were a much loved child.

'You are such a beautiful boy,' Renée crooned as
her right hand continued its rhythmic petting. Her left
arm was curled round the horse's neck, with the side
of her head resting against his glossy black mane.
'Ward says there's no sign of that shin soreness coming back and you'll be ready for your first race soon.
And he says you'll win. I did tell him that you might
be a little nervous to begin with and we shouldn't

expect too much too soon, but he said you didn't have a nervous bone in your body. He said you were a born racehorse. A potential champion. Oh, I do so wish you were all mine, my darling. But I suppose one third of you is better than nothing.'

Rico didn't know whether he felt jealous of the horse on the receiving end of Renée's caresses. Or of Ward Jackman. It sounded as if the man said one hell of a lot more to Renée than he did to him, or anyone else for that matter. Could it be that Renée's relationship with Jackman extended beyond trainer and owner?

Suddenly, Renée's BMW being parked right outside Ward's front gate took on a different and more ominous meaning. Maybe she hadn't arrived first today. Maybe her car had been there all night...

Rico swallowed the bile which leap into his throat and tried to look at this appalling idea more rationally and without panic. There'd never been a hint of intimacy shown between them that he'd noticed. No telling glances, or untoward touching.

But their being lovers would certainly explain the uncharacteristic amount of chit-chat which obviously had been going on between them about Ebony Fire. Even the most taciturn men were prone to pillow talk.

The thought of Renée sleeping with the ruggedly handsome horse trainer stabbed deep into Rico's heart. His fists curled over by his side, his nails digging into his palms. Theoretical lovers were a whole different ball game to an in-your-face, flesh-and-blood one. If what Rico suspected was true, then it was no wonder she never brought a boyfriend to the races. He was already there!

He stared at the way she was cuddling and petting

the horse, but his brain didn't see Ebony Fire as the recipient of her caresses any longer. His mind's eye was picturing Ward Jackman, naked and aroused, beneath her hands.

A violent shudder ran down Rico's spine.

The colt suddenly swung his head Rico's way as he spotted him standing there at the stable door and neighed a welcome to his new visitor. Renée whirled, her eyes widening when she saw who that new visitor was.

For a few moments her usual composure seemed to desert her, her body language showing agitation as she hurried over to the stable door, the horse hot on her heels.

'What on earth are *you* doing here?' she snapped as she wrenched open the bottom half of the stable door and slipped out of the stall, quickly closing the door behind her before the colt could follow. 'Don't you usually go home to the family on the first Sunday of the month?'

The way she said the word, *'family'*, suggested he was a member of the Mafia, rather than the son of an honest, hard-working market gardener.

'And hello to you too,' Rico returned, impressed at how cool he sounded in the face of the jealousy and fury raging inside him. 'The thing is, my dear Renée, I just couldn't go another day without a dose of your charming company,' he added in a mocking tone which masked the truth behind his words.

She totally ignored him as she concentrated on shoving the bolt home on the door before finally raising cool green eyes to his. 'In that case, why weren't you at the races yesterday?'

Rico smiled. 'Aah, so you noticed I wasn't there. I'm flattered.'

'Don't be. I had a very pleasant afternoon. I picked several winners as well.'

'In that case, why are you so sour today? Or is that always your disposition around me?'

Rico could feel his tongue running away with him, along with any hope he had of Renée ever accepting an invitation to go out on a date.

Not that he was going to ask her now. Not until he discovered what was going on between her and Jackman. No man liked to make a total fool of himself, not even when that man was as desperate as he was.

His gaze swept over the object of that desperation, trying not to ogle the way the tight camel-coloured trousers she was wearing hugged every inch of her long, slender legs. Her neat white T-shirt was equally snug-fitting and showed more bust than he realised she had. Either that, or she was wearing a padded bra.

No, no padding, he realised on a second glance. Damn, no bra at all! Her nipples were starkly outlined against the thin white cotton, as long and hard as bullets.

Maybe their erect state was due to her being cold— the day still hadn't warmed up much. Or maybe their condition was the result of her having spent all night in Jackman's bed.

His stomach crunched down hard at the image of the other man sucking on Renée's nipples. He could not bear it. He should leave. Right now, before he did or said something he would really regret.

But he couldn't.

'Would you mind if I asked you a personal question?' he grated out, struggling not to sound the way he was feeling.

'Would it stop you if I did?' she flung back at him.

'No.'

'I didn't think so.'

'Are you and Ward lovers?' he demanded to know, his eyes glued to hers.

There was no doubt her face registered shock, her finely arched brows arching even further over rapidly blinking eyes, her red-glossed mouth dropping slightly open.

Her recovery was swift, however, with her face resuming its characteristically self-contained, slightly superior expression. Ignoring him again for a few moments, she bent to pick up the black leather jacket and matching bag which he hadn't noticed sitting on the ground next to the stable wall. The movement swung her smooth curtain of thick, shoulder-length brown hair across her high cheekbones, momentarily hiding her face from him. When she straightened it fell back into perfect place, a testament to the expertise of her hairdresser. Tilting up her chin slightly, she fixed her slanting green eyes on his own eyes, her gaze cool and steady.

'Why do you ask? Has someone said something about us?'

'No. But I heard you talking to Blackie here just now and it sounded like you were pretty chummy with Ward. Let's face it, it's hard to get two words out of that man at the best of times, but he seems to have told you plenty about the horse's progress.'

'So you jumped to the conclusion that he told me in bed.'

'Well, did he?'

'I don't think that's any of your business,' she said quite coldly, and turned back to start stroking Blackie's head once more.

'I'm making it my business,' he bit out.

'Why?' she said indifferently, not even bothering to glance his way. 'What's it to you who I sleep with?'

'I don't like you sleeping with Jackman,' he ground out.

Now she did stop stroking the horse to look at him, her expression curious. 'But why?'

What could he say? I don't like you sleeping with *any* man. I want you in my bed and my bed only.

She would laugh in his face.

His pride simply could not stand that degree of humiliation.

'He's the syndicate's trainer,' he snapped instead. 'I don't like the idea of you getting inside information which should be shared with all the partners.'

She gave a small, dry laugh. 'Typical. I should have known the reason would be something like that. For your information, I'm *not* sleeping with Ward. If you had any brains at all, or any powers of observation, you'd know that he and Lisa are madly in love. She's even moved in with him. The only reason Ward talks to me more than you is because he knows I genuinely love my horses. I'm not just in racing for the status, or the socialising. Satisfied now?'

When she went to move away, he grabbed her arm. She stiffened and shot him a look which would have shriveled a lesser man. Rico's fingers tightened.

'Why do you dislike me so much?' he demanded to know. 'What have I ever done to you?'

She stared down at the hand circled on her arm till he let her go, at which point she actually shuddered.

Rico knew then that she would never go out with him, let alone go to bed with him. Not willingly. He repelled her for some reason.

It was the most appalling realisation of his life, worse than discovering Jasmine was a gold-digger. Much worse than anything he could imagine.

Now *he* was the one who shuddered. But not visibly. Inside. Deep, deep inside.

'You don't want me to answer those questions,' she replied tartly. 'Trust me on that.'

'But I do,' he ground out. 'Trust me on *that*.'

Her green eyes frosted over further, if that was possible. 'Very well. I'll tell you. The reason I dislike you so much is because you represent everything I despise in the male sex. You're selfish and self-centred and appallingly shallow. You say you want substance in your life but you continually choose shadows. You also make snap judgements about people without ever looking beneath the surface. When I think of how you nearly ruined Charles's marriage...'

Her top lip curled up in contempt and Rico cringed. OK, so he'd made a terrible mistake in accusing Dominique of being the same kind of heartless gold-digger Jasmine had been. But the evidence *had* seemed damning at the time.

'All because you couldn't see past your own pathetic marital experience,' Renée continued caustically. 'Like I said, selfish and shallow. Of course, most really good-looking men are tarred with the same brush. You imagine that you're so irresistible, just because you were born with a great body and loads of sex appeal. You think I don't know that your arrogant Italian nose is put out of joint because I don't swoon every time you come into the room? Or that you're seriously irritated by the fact I can play poker better than you can? I might have more respect for you, Rico Mandretti, if just *once* you behaved with some depth and sensitivity. But no, you just keep on keeping on in your usual superficial playboy fashion, acting like a spoiled brat when you don't get your way!'

By now her voice had risen slightly and Rico cast a desperate glance around, relieved to see that Neil had finished his hosing down and was nowhere in sight.

'But most pathetic of all,' Renée swept on, regardless, 'is the way you go from one blonde bimbo to the next, then bemoan the fact you haven't got what Charles has got. Grow up, Rico. Get a life, and a nice girl for a wife. *Have* that family you claim you want. Then maybe I might grow to like you. No, maybe not,' she added scornfully. 'Liking you is something I'll never do. But at least I'd have some respect for you.'

At last, her tirade was finished. And so was Rico.

He had never been on the end of such a brutal character assassination in all his life. Not even Jasmine at her most venomous had managed to make him feel so utterly worthless.

He could have lashed back, he supposed. Could have torn strips off Renée's own less than perfect past. But somehow, he had a feeling that might backfire on him as well. Though goodness knew how. No one would ever convince him she'd married that old geezer for love. Still, possibly money hadn't been her motive. Maybe his believing her a gold-digger was one of those snap judgements she'd referred to.

'I did warn you,' she stated brusquely when he just stood there, silent and shattered. 'Don't make me feel guilty for speaking the truth. Don't you dare! It's not as though you give a damn what I think, anyway. Men like you don't give a damn about anyone but themselves.'

And with an angry toss of her hair she pushed past him and stalked off.

Well at least she thinks I'm good-looking, Rico thought bitterly as he watched her go. Clearly, she's repelled more by my characterless character than my great body or my arrogant Italian nose. That was something, wasn't it?

'Yeah, right, Rico,' he muttered bleakly and, sliding his hands deeply back into his trouser pockets, he trudged back across the still blessedly deserted courtyard, murmured a desolate goodbye to Jed at the gate then headed wearily for his car, and home.

CHAPTER FOUR

CHARLES glanced across the card table at an unusually quiet Renée, then sidewards at a very grim-faced Rico, and wondered what on earth had happened between those two during the past week. They'd been in good form last Friday night, hitting off each other with their usual savage but highly entertaining wit.

But tonight was a different story entirely. Tonight they were both tight-lipped and tight-fisted. The pots so far had been small, the betting abysmal. Neither Rico nor Renée seemed interested in trying to outbluff each other the way they usually did. Rico was particularly dull. Even when he had a fairly good hand, he didn't raise the stakes to his usual daring degree.

All in all, it was turning out to be one of the most boring poker nights Charles had ever sat through. He would much rather have stayed home with Dominique. Frankly, he couldn't wait for the evening to end. Yet it was only ten-twenty. At least they'd be stopping soon for supper.

'It's your turn to deal, Charles,' Ali reminded him. 'We'll make this the last hand before supper.'

'Good,' Charles said.

Rico agreed. All he wanted to do was finish this torture and get out of here. With a weary-sounding sigh, he started picking up the five cards Charles had dealt to him. The first was the queen of hearts. The second, the jack of hearts. When the third turned out to be the king of hearts, his own heart gave a little flutter. When the fourth proved to be the ace of hearts, his heart ceased to beat altogether.

Holy hell!

At that point, mathematical probability told Rico all he could seriously hope his last card to be was one more heart of any kind, giving him a flush. Or possibly a ten—again of any suit—completing a straight. To think that it could possibly be the ten of hearts, completing a royal flush, was a million-to-one chance. He'd heard of it happening but never seen it, let alone experienced it personally.

His fingertips clipped the edge of the table as he went to pick up his last card. Renée's eyes immediately flicked his way. Before Rico could think better of it, his head turned and their gazes connected.

It was the first time he'd looked straight at her all night, other than when she'd first walked into the presidential suite right on eight o'clock, looking elegantly sexy in cream woollen trousers and a pale green twin set.

He *had* been thinking about her constantly since last Sunday's fiasco, wondering what to do about his escalating frustration. And he'd come here tonight, still not sure what action to take. His body's immediate and involuntary response to just the sight of her had swiftly made up his mind.

This was going to be his last night playing poker with the merry widow. Charles and Ali would have to find someone else. He would opt out of the racing syndicate as well. On top of that, he aimed to leave Sydney and go overseas for a while. He'd been offered the opportunity to take his show on the road to

Italy. He intended to do just that. He had to get right away from this scene before he self-destructed.

His decisions, though sensible, had depressed him, and the evening's card-playing so far had passed in a fog. But the four cards he now held in his hand could not help but set the adrenaline flowing in any poker player.

This time, when he looked at Renée, his excitement was not of the sexual kind.

Her smile, when it came, startled him. Was it an apology? A peace offering?

No, he swiftly realised. It was far too wry, and knowing. Clearly, she had sensed his sudden tension, and was waiting to see his reaction to his last card. Rico noted that she was already holding all five of her cards, so she knew the state of her own hand.

How cold-blooded, and clever she was!

His eyes dropped away from hers, but he felt her watch him closely as he picked up his fifth and last card.

Did he manage to hide his reaction? He believed so, but every internal muscle he owned stiffened with the effort of keeping his hands still and his expression poker-faced. After all, how often did you pick up the one card which gave you not just a great hand, but also an unbeatable one?

Unbeatable!

His heart thudded heavily in his chest as he battled to remain outwardly composed. Blood pounded through his temples. His mouth went dry.

'How many cards do you want, Rico?' Charles asked him somewhat impatiently.

Quite deliberately, he hesitated, before relaxing back into his chair and adopting an attitude of over-confidence. This was not how he usually acted when he had a really good hand. His aim in adopting such a manner was to confuse his opposition, to convince the others he was bluffing, otherwise they would all fold and he wouldn't win a single cent.

And what a criminal waste that would be!

'I think I'll sit on what I've got,' he said, tone smug, mouth twitching at the corner.

Ali frowned over at him, dark eyes puzzled. Rico smiled back at him, thinking that he would enjoy taking a few thousand of Ali's oil-rich millions off him. The trouble was Ali was no fool. He rarely lost much at the card table. Would he smell a rat and fold, regardless?

'So Enrico is alive tonight after all,' Ali murmured, and discarded three cards. Charles dealt him three more. Unfortunately, Ali didn't look thrilled with what he picked up, which meant he probably wasn't going to take part in the betting, no matter what he thought Rico was up to. Ali wouldn't have shown his disgust if he'd been planning on bluffing.

Now it was Renée's turn. 'I'll sit too,' she said in that soft, silky voice which Rico found impossible to read. Sometimes she was bluffing. At other times, she held a full house, or at least three of a kind.

No matter this time. Whatever she had, she could not possibly win. Rico's body fizzed with elation as he looked over at her.

I'm going to go out a winner here tonight, madam, Rico thought with a savagery born of a severely bruised male pride. I hope you've got a full house. Or even four of a kind. Either that, or I hope you think I'm bluffing and you bet every cent you've got.

'I'm taking two,' Charles said, which suggested he

could be holding three of a kind. But possibly not. Charles often sat on a pair and a high card. He seemed pleased with what he drew. But that could mean anything. Charles was a very sneaky poker player when he was on his game.

Rico was right about Ali. He dropped out of the hand straight away. Renée stayed in, continually raising the stakes. Rico did the same. Charles folded when the pot reached the six-figure mark.

'This is too hot for me,' he said as he closed his hand and placed it face down on the table. 'You two can fight it out.'

'I think Rico should save his money and fold now too,' Renée advised coolly. 'Unless, of course, he enjoys losing. I suspect he must, the way he's been playing tonight.'

It was the wrong thing to say, especially with Rico holding the cards he was holding, and feeling the feelings he'd been feeling all week.

Suddenly, his winning Renée's money wasn't enough. He wanted to strike at her pride, as she had shattered his last Sunday.

The sheer wickedness of the wager which sprang into his mind sent his heartbeat into overdrive. If Renée wasn't bluffing—and he suspected she wasn't—she would not be able to resist his proposal.

And then she was would be his. *His*, where he'd always wanted her. In his bed.

Just the thought of it gave him an instant erection.

'If you're so confident,' he said smoothly despite the dark excitement racing through his veins, 'how about we raise the stakes?'

'You mean increase the maximum bet?' she returned, her finely plucked brows drawing together in a frown.

'No. I was thinking we could wager for something other than money.'

Her head jerked back, long eyelashes blinking rapidly. 'Like what?'

'Yes, like what?' Charles piped up.

'Whatever we fancy. Renée can choose something she wants which I can give or buy her. And vice versa. Anything at all.'

Her eyes flashed scornfully. 'I can't think of *anything* you could give me that I couldn't buy for myself.'

'*Can't* you? I got the impression at the open day last Sunday that that wasn't the case...'

He locked eyes with hers and saw the penny drop. His share of Ebony Fire. She wanted that all right. He could guess what was going on in her devious mind. If she won his third, it would be relatively easy to buy out Charles' share. He was already losing interest in the syndicate. Then she would have her dearest wish. To own *all* of her precious colt.

Rico knew Renée would not be able to resist the temptation. She would agree to the bet and fall right into his trap.

'I'm not so sure about this,' Charles said, ever the gentleman. 'It doesn't sound right.'

'Mind your own business, Charles,' Renée snapped, showing Rico that she was already on the slippery slide to hell. 'This is between Rico and myself. So how do you suggest we go about this?'

'We write our heart's desire down on separate pieces of paper,' Rico suggested. 'Then we put each in its own envelope and place them both next to the pot. We then show our cards at the same time and the winner takes the pot. The loser is then handed the winner's envelope and has to deliver whatever the winner wants.'

'So we don't have to say up front what we're actually betting for,' Renée said, her expression thoughtful. 'It's a secret.'

'Yes. It's more exciting that way, don't you think?'

'What happens to the loser's envelope?' she asked him, green eyes narrowed.

'She—or he—can take it back, if they like, sight unseen by the other.'

Her frown deepened. 'I just can't imagine what you could possibly want from me.'

'Maybe it's the same thing you want from me.'

She stared hard at him. 'Maybe,' she said at last. 'But somehow, I doubt it. Still, it might be...interesting...to find out.'

'Provided I win, of course,' Rico added, pretending that the result wasn't a foregone conclusion. 'If I don't, I'll certainly be taking *my* envelope back.'

Her eyes shot him a look which he would have given anything to read. But that had always been her skill, hiding the truth from him when she wanted to. That was why he never knew when she was bluffing or not.

'Let's get the paper and envelopes, then,' she said crisply.

'I'm still not sure I like this idea at all,' Charles grumbled.

'Why not?' Rico returned with a shrug of his broad shoulders. 'What's the harm? It's just a bit of fun.'

'I suppose so,' Charles said grudgingly. 'By the

look of you tonight, you certainly could do with some lightening up.'

'But we won't make a habit of this kind of wager,' Ali inserted with his usual authority, never liking things to become personal at his card table. 'This is a one-off. *James*,' he called to the butler who was at that moment preparing supper over in the adjoining sitting room. 'Bring Mr Mandretti a notepad, two pens and two envelopes.'

'Yes, Your Highness,' the butler replied and walked over to the writing desk in the corner of the sitting room, where he gathered the required objects and delivered them with his usual aplomb.

Rico ripped off the top page of the hotel notepad and handed the rest of the pad to Renée, along with a Biro and an envelope. She wrote quickly, clearly knowing exactly what she wanted to ask for. Rico, however, found himself suddenly in a quandary. How much to ask for? One night with her? Two? Or every night for a week?

Not enough, he decided darkly as his flesh grew even harder. Not nearly enough. So he put his pen to paper and wrote.

'You are now my mistress for a month, starting tonight.'

His hands trembled slightly as he folded the sheet of paper and shoved it into the remaining envelope. On the outside he scrawled his name, then tossed it on top of Renée's envelope.

Yes, on top, he thought with another overwhelming rush of desire. That was where he was going to be every night for the next month. On top of Renée. Except when he ordered her to take that position her-self. Mistresses could be ordered into whatever position or activity which took their lover's fancy. That was their role in life, wasn't it, to keep the men who kept them sexually satisfied, to accede to their every demand?

Of course, Rico understood he would have to pay for the privilege. Mistresses did not come much cheaper than gold-digging wives. But it would give him great pleasure to spend money on Renée. To shower her with jewels and dress her in designer clothes. She wore trousers far too often for his liking, despite the fact they suited her tall, willowy figure, and made her lovely long legs look even longer.

Still, he wanted to see what she looked like in soft, floaty dresses and low-cut evening gowns and black satin nighties with tiny straps which yielded to a mere flick of a finger. He also wanted to see what she looked like wearing nothing at all except that subtly musky perfume which sometimes drove him mad. But most of all he wanted to see what she looked like when she came.

That would be the ultimate triumph, and the best salve for his male pride, to make her lose control, to watch her mouth fall open as he listened to her moans of unexpected ecstasy.

Rico knew that if there was one talent he had, and which had not been God-given, it was his skill in the bedroom. Admittedly, those naturally born good looks which Renée had scorned last Sunday *had* made it easy for him to get women into his bed. Frankly, the opposite sex had been coming on to him in droves since he was fourteen.

But, as was his nature, he hadn't been content to just "Do it." Rico never saw the point of doing anything unless he did it to the best of his ability. So he'd made a point of learning everything which could be learned about giving and receiving sexual pleasure. He'd set out to discover what women really wanted in the lovemaking department. Gradually, he'd uncovered their secret desires and acted upon them, with great success. Jasmine might have married him mainly for his money, but she had certainly enjoyed herself in their marital bed.

Rico was confident Renée would enjoy herself with him just as much, once he got past her defences.

Because, of course, she wasn't going to be pleased when she read his demand. She was, in fact, sure to be downright furious.

Too bad. A bet was a bet. You had to pay up. In full. Renée knew that.

Rico didn't doubt the merry widow would deliver. But not happily, or willingly. At least, not to begin with…

His challenge was to bring her round, to make her see that being his mistress was a very pleasurable way to spend the next month. The thought of seducing her totally to his sexual will was almost as exciting as looking at the unbelievable hand he was holding.

'Come on, then,' Charles said impatiently. 'Let's see your hands.'

Charles' speaking at this juncture jolted Rico. He'd forgotten what his best friend's reaction would be once his less than gentlemanly demand was made public. Charles would be shocked, and disapproving. Ali, not so much, Rico imagined. His ideas on women and sex were along more primitive lines. Whenever Ali met a young lady he fancied at the races here in Sydney, he often invited her to accompany him home here to the presidential suite for the night, then on to his property for the following week. But she was always returned the following Friday. And was never invited again.

Despite his one-week affairs being common knowledge around Sydney's racing set, he still had no trouble finding willing companions. Frankly, Ali had even less trouble getting women to share his bed—even on this temporary basis—than Rico. Jasmine had once described the Arab prince as sex on legs.

Of course, his billions added considerable impetus to his sex appeal, as it did with all seriously wealthy men. But if the women who went with Ali thought they would ever catch him for a husband, then they were sorely mistaken. Ali had once confided in Rico he had no interest in marriage. Or having children. His horses were his children and women were just a pleasant diversion.

No. Ali would not be shocked by Rico's demand. Not one iota.

Charles, however, was another matter.

Too late to worry about that, however. It was time to put his cards on the table. Time to claim his prize.

CHAPTER FIVE

'TOGETHER, then?' Rico suggested, too excited now to care what anybody thought.

Renée's shoulders lifted in a seemingly nonchalant shrug but he detected a flash of something in her eyes. Surely not panic. Was she afraid, suddenly, that she might lose?

Her hand trembled slightly as she placed her cards down just before his. So she *was* worried.

She had every right to be, came the devilish thought when he saw her cards. Four nines was a good hand. But not nearly good enough.

'Hope you're not bluffing, pal,' Charles said as Rico exposed his own incredible hand.

Renée sucked in sharply whilst Charles openly gaped.

'My God!' he exclaimed. 'A royal routine. You know, I've never seen one of those before.'

'I have,' Ali said drily. 'How wicked of you, Enrico, to trick Renée into such a wager with such a hand.'

'Renée didn't have to agree,' Rico retorted, his elation refusing to give way to guilt. 'It was up to her to gauge what kind of hand I was holding. She should have known I wasn't bluffing.'

'I did,' Renée said, composed once more. 'I just didn't realise your hand was unbeatable. I did have pretty good cards myself, you know.'

Rico frowned over at her. She should have been more disappointed. More angry with him.

Still, she hadn't read his demand yet. What would happen when she did? If Rico was any judge of character at all—something Renée insisted he wasn't—he would bet that she wouldn't make a scene. She would be cool and controlled, till she got him in private. *Then*, she'd let him have it.

In a perverse kind of way, he was looking forward to that moment. The only thing about last Sunday that he'd enjoyed was seeing her in a temper over him.

Heated dislike was much preferable to cold uninterest. Her admission that she thought him physically attractive had not been forgotten, either. Hell, he was depending on it!

When she reached for the two envelopes, his stomach suddenly twisted into the most awful knot. But she bypassed the one which had his name on it and picked up the other one.

'I can have this back now, can't I?' she said with a saucy tilt of her chin. 'That was the deal. The loser gets to keep his—or her—heart's desire secret.'

'It's no secret from me,' Rico snapped, irritated by the delay in her opening *his* envelope. 'I know exactly what you asked for.'

'You only think you do,' came her cryptic comment.

Rico could not believe it. Even in his moment of triumph, she had to make some smart remark which would distract him and make him wonder. He wished now that he hadn't made that particular condition of the bet. He would have preferred to see for himself exactly what she'd written. As much as he was pretty sure that she would have asked for his share of Ebony Fire, now he'd never know for certain.

And she'd never tell him. He knew Renée well enough to know that!

'This is all getting too much for me,' Charles grumbled. 'Just open Rico's envelope, for pity's sake, and let's see what he wants. But I hope you've got plenty of money, Renée, because with that hand Rico could have asked for the world!'

'I doubt our Italian friend would have asked for anything which could be bought,' Ali said quietly and with his usual insight. 'I suspect it will be something only Renée could give him.'

'My thoughts, exactly,' Renée remarked, coolly taking her time putting her envelope away in the handbag she always kept at her feet before finally picking up the envelope with Rico's name on it. 'Are we right, Rico?' she asked, a small, knowing smile playing around her mouth as she turned her gaze on to him.

Rico battled to stop his face from burning, a mammoth effort considering his body was on fire and his brain besieged by the most humiliating of realisations. She knew. *Knew* what he'd asked for. In essence, anyway. Ali suspected as well.

Had he been so obvious these last couple of years? Had they all known how much he'd wanted her, how he'd sat there every Friday night in a torment of desire and need?

Charles had guessed Rico's supposedly secret feelings for the merry widow some time back, but Charles was his best friend and privy to Rico's confidences. Rico hadn't realised the other two had known what he was enduring as well. It was mortifying in the extreme.

Once again, she'd struck at his pride. He tried not to glower at her, tried to keep his face from betraying the resentment raging within him. But he could never hide his feelings the way she could. He could feel his eyes blazing and his heart pounding with fury. He vowed to make her pay, in the only way he could.

Some time during the next month he'd reduce her to begging for him. He'd make her whimper with need, and moan with desire. He might even make her fall in love with him!

What a delicious revenge that would be for the way she'd constantly belittled him over the years; to have the merry widow surrender her soul to him, as well as her body.

Even as she opened his envelope, he already knew what to expect. No visible reaction whatsoever. No shock. No anger. Not on the outside, anyway. She would protect *her* pride at all costs. To hell with his, though.

'Well, well, well,' was all she said, with just the slightest raising of her right eyebrow, the one she always cocked when she was being her usual sarcastic self. 'I'm surprised, Rico. If that was all you wanted, you only had to ask. You didn't have to wait for a million-to-one chance to have your heart's desire.'

Rico gritted his teeth and willed the angry flush away. 'You mean you would have said yes if I'd just asked?'

'Asked what?' Charles demanded to know. 'What has he asked for, damn it? Or aren't we allowed to know that either?'

'Don't get your dander up, Charles,' Renée said

soothingly. 'Of course you can know. It's nothing worth hiding. Rico just wants me to go out with him.'

Rico could not deny her answer stunned him. He'd been sure she'd drop him right in it. But then the truth surfaced. Of course! She was protecting *her* pride again. She didn't want the others to know what she'd be doing for the next month.

'But that doesn't make any sense,' Charles said with more than a touch of bewilderment in his voice. 'If you wanted to ask Renée out, then why didn't you just ask, like she said?'

'Because he didn't want to risk her saying no,' Ali explained. 'No man likes to be rejected.'

'Renée wouldn't have said no,' Charles said firmly. 'Would you, Renée?'

'Absolutely not, Charles,' Renée returned in that seemingly polite but cleverly mocking tone Rico knew only too well. 'How could I possibly have resisted Rico's charm?'

'I *have* asked her out before,' Rico pointed out through gritted teeth, his temper only just under control.

'Only to family affairs,' she countered. 'Not on an intimate, one-on-one basis.'

When she said one-on-one, her eyes met his and Rico could have sworn that he glimpsed a glitter of excitement, not mockery, in their depths.

No, no, he had to be mistaken. She couldn't possibly *want* to sleep with him. OK, so he *was* bargaining on her not finding him physically repulsive, but she'd made it quite clear last Sunday she didn't like him one little bit. He'd be the last man on earth she'd choose for her lover.

'Dominique is going to be tickled pink,' Charles

said with a delighted smile. 'You two won't be able to refuse her dinner invitations in future.'

'We're just going out a few times, Charles,' Rico pointed out. 'See if we can get along. Don't make plans for our future just yet.'

'Surely we could manage one little dinner party, Rico,' Renée shocked him by saying. 'I still feel guilty over refusing Dominique's last invitation for us to go to dinner. Tell her to give me a call, Charles, and we'll set a date soon.'

Rico sat there, smiling his agreement on the outside but fuming on the inside. He didn't want to have to pretend to be a real partner to Renée in front of his friends. That was not his plan. She was to be kept for the darkness of the night, to be used strictly for his private pleasure. When he took her out, it would be for drinks and dirty dancing in dimly lit clubs, dressed as only a mistress would be dressed. He didn't want to have to play the gentleman. Not for a single moment.

Somehow, he would wangle his way out of that dinner invitation.

'James has supper ready,' Ali announced, and began to rise from his chair.

Supper on poker nights was nothing heavy, just a tasty selection of sandwiches and pastries and coffee, all set up on the large coffee-table where the four of them could sit on the surrounding seating and serve themselves. Except for the coffee part. James did the honours there, then hovered to one side with the coffee-pot, ready for top-ups.

Rarely did supper last longer than half an hour, the drinking and eating usually interspersed by trips to the powder room. Renée always used the last ten minutes or so to have a couple of cigarettes on the balcony that came off the dining area, a hangover from her modelling days, when she'd used smoking to keep her weight down, one of her few revelations about her past.

That night, she bolted her first cup of coffee down, Rico noticed. Didn't touch any food then carried a second cup of coffee out onto the balcony. He would have followed her out there if Charles hadn't kept blathering on about how he still couldn't believe that hand and that bet.

'Hell, Rico, you could have asked for anything. Anything at all. But all you wanted was a date. I didn't realise you were such a romantic.'

'All men are romantics,' Ali said. 'If they meet the right woman. Unfortunately, that's where the problem often lies. Meeting the right woman.' He placed his empty coffee-cup down, then waved the butler back when he stepped forward to refill. Ali could drink coffee with the same gusto Rico downed his Chianti. 'No more tonight, James. I'll be back shortly, my friends, then we can get back to the card table.'

When Ali left the room and Charles pulled out his cellphone to ring Dominique, claiming he couldn't wait to get home to tell her about Rico's hand and his amazing wager, Rico used the opportunity to join Renée out onto the balcony.

As he passed the outdoor table on which she'd put her bag and her coffee-cup, Rico noticed that the ash-tray sitting in the middle was filled with recently burnt paper. The realisation that she'd hurried out here to physically destroy her own heart's desire piqued Rico's curiosity further, but he determined not to mention it. He also determined not to weaken and let her off the hook, no matter how much guilt was currently swirling in his stomach.

The sight of her leaning against the railing in an attitude close to defeat sparked even more guilt within him. How can you possibly go through with this, Rico Mandretti? he asked himself.

The answer was a very complex one. But, in a nutshell, he didn't have a choice. Having her at least once was a compulsion, a necessity. Expecting her to accommodate him for a month, however, was definitely beyond the pale.

'What are you thinking?' he asked as he leant against the railing next to her.

She didn't look his way, or answer him, just kept on dragging on her cigarette.

'One night,' he grated out at last, regretting the words even as he spoke them. 'I'll reduce the bet to one night.'

Slowly she exhaled, then turned to face him, her expression haughty and scornful. '*Pity*, Rico? From *you*? I'm surprised. But sorry, darling, I must refuse your gallant gesture. A bet is a bet. You demanded I be your mistress for a month, so your mistress for a month I will be. Not a day less. Not a day more.'

Her contrariness jolted him. Was this her pride still talking, or did she have some other secret agenda? Whatever the case, experience had taught Rico never to try to second-guess Renée, so he just shrugged.

'Fine by me.' Far be it from him to lessen her sentence. She'd made her bed now. Let her lie in it.

'You might think that tonight,' she replied. 'You might think differently in a month's time.'

'Is that a threat, Renée? Or a challenge?'

'It's a promise. I don't just dislike you now, Rico.
I despise you.'

'If you despise me so much, then why didn't you
tell Charles what I really asked of you? Why save me
with a lie?'

'Oh, good God!' she exclaimed impatiently. 'I
didn't lie for *you*. I just didn't want Charles to find
out what an out-and-out bastard his best friend is.'

'Why would you bother?'

'Because the foolish man likes you, that's why.
And I like him. Why should he be upset by any of
this? You've caused him enough hurt this year, don't
you think? This battle is strictly between us, and
that's how it's going to stay.'

'Battle? That's an odd word to use.'

'I think it's very appropriate. We are at war, you
and I. We have been for a long time.'

'Maybe it's time we stopped, then. Maybe it's time
we made love, not war.'

'Make *love*?' she scoffed. 'You must be insane.
You don't want to make love to me any more than I
want to make love with you. You want revenge, that's
all, for what I said to you last Sunday.'

Rico saw with a sudden and quite blinding insight
that revenge *wasn't* his first and deepest wish where
she was concerned. He would have much preferred
her to like him, and respect him, and, yes, desire him
for the man he was.

But he knew that wasn't about to happen.

So he wasn't going to belittle himself further by
putting his stupid heart on his sleeve.

'Believe what you will, Renée. I will be booking
us a room here in the hotel as soon as the evening's
poker is over. I will expect you to accompany me.

And to stay the whole night. Given you don't want dear Charles to know what an out-and-out bastard I am, then I suggest you meet me in the lobby, *after* he's left the hotel.'

She didn't even turn a hair. Not visibly, anyway. Rico began to wonder if she was a living, breathing woman, or some evil robot designed by the devil and sent to earth to torment and torture fools like him.

'Fine by me,' she said, echoing his dismissive words earlier. 'Just one question before we go back inside. There are mistresses, and mistresses, Rico. What, exactly, will you be requiring? The I'll-do-anything-you-want-when-you-want-it sex-kitten type of mistress, or the seriously kinky, black-leather-wearing, whip-wielding variety?'

Rico was truly taken aback. Then slightly intrigued. 'What if I chose the latter?'

Her smile was pure ice. 'I'd be most gratified. I've always thought a good beating or two was what you needed most in the world.'

Rico couldn't help it. He laughed. This was the Renée who aroused him most. The sarcastic spitting cat. 'Then perhaps it's just as well that that scenario doesn't appeal to me,' he replied, still smiling. 'I would like to survive this month with my skin intact.'

'Ah, yes, but what about your soul?' she countered snakily. 'Do you really believe you can go through with this and live with yourself afterwards?'

For a moment, his conscience *was* pricked. Rico understood full well that what he was doing was wrong. But he was way beyond right and wrong where this woman was concerned.

'You're quite right,' he said, feigning a contrite face and enjoying her momentary look of surprise. 'I have no doubt I will feel very badly afterwards. But I can always run along to Confession if needs be. Come along, my dear Mrs Selinsky,' he went on, abruptly whipping the cigarette out of her hand. 'It's time to return to the card table.' He stalked over and stabbed the cigarette to death in the still smouldering ashtray before lifting glittering eyes to hers once more.

'Not that I'll be able to put my mind back on poker. I'll be too busy picturing as a—how did you describe your role for the next month?—a you'll-do-anything-I-want-when-I-want-it sex-kitten type of mistress. The mind boggles how you're going to manage it, given you despise me so much. But I recall reading once that models have to be marvelous actresses as well as clothes-horses. So just do what I'm sure you did very well when you were strutting your stuff on the cat-walk, *and* when you were married to Mr Selinsky. *Act.*'

CHAPTER SIX

'WHATEVER possessed you to book one of the honeymoon suites?' she said quite angrily as he unlocked the door.

Rico gave her a satisfied look. She was nervous, he realised. Good. Because he was nervous, too. All that bravado he'd displayed on the balcony earlier had dissipated during the remaining hour's poker, leaving him in a right royal mess.

'Don't complain,' he advised brusquely. Or explain, he told himself. She doesn't need to know that you didn't want to take her to one of the standard rooms where you'd taken Leanne; that you'd wanted something special for their first night together, romantic fool that he was.

The lights came on the second he slotted his keycard into the gizmo next to the door. Not bright, overhead lights. Subtle wall-lights and lamps.

Renée's sharply sucked-in breath was an echo of what Rico thought as he glanced around. Wow. It was romantic all right.

'I don't believe this,' Renée said as she strode across the black marble foyer and through an ornate archway into a sitting room which looked like something out of *The Arabian Nights*. Rico followed, equally startled by the decor.

Crimson carpet underfoot. Walls papered in the deepest blue. Ceiling covered with draped swathes of black silk shot with gold. Incredible all right.

The furniture and furnishings were equally exotic. Aquamarine silk curtains adorned the large picture window, each fall tied back with matching sashes, decorated with huge gold tassels which hung to the floor. The low curved sofas were just as colourful, arranged around a black lacquered circular coffee-table on which sat a gold-plated ice-bucket filled with the obligatory bottle of chilled champagne. Next to it were two gilt-edged crystal glasses and a platter of cheeses and fresh fruits which must have been dispatched and delivered whilst they were riding up in the lift. The Regency was renowned for its swift room service.

'This is like something out of fantasy-land,' Renée said drily as she put her handbag down on a black lacquered side table and walked over to another wider archway on the right.

'My God,' she gasped as she entered the bedroom, Rico still trailing in her wake.

If the sitting room was out of fantasy-land then the bedroom surpassed it. The carpet in there was emerald, and thick as lush grass. Rico could only imagine how it would feel in bare feet. The walls were papered in what looked like silver foil. The four-poster black lacquered bed was raised on a platform in the centre of the room and totally surrounded by gauzy white curtains, the kind that dressed the bedroom settings in the desert film epics of the fifties. The quilt was white satin shot with silver, with a countless number of matching pillows and scatter cushions leaning against the curved headboard. The ceiling, Rico noted with raised eyebrows, was totally mirrored.

The desk clerk had said something about all the

honeymoon suites being themed but Rico had been too agitated at the time to listen properly.

Both their gazes finally left the bed to scan the rest of the room, simultaneously landing on the two naked statues that flanked the archway through which they'd just walked. Lifelike in size, both were made in pale grey marble and both were blatantly erotic.

It was impossible to look at them without thinking of sex. An already painfully erect Rico didn't need any further stimulation. Or any further delay.

Renée kept staring at the impassioned carvings and didn't hear Rico come up behind her. She jumped when he curled his hands over her shoulders. But she didn't say a word in protest. His hands tightened as he pulled her back against him, bringing just the whisper of a moan from her lips.

'Sexy, aren't they?' he murmured into her hair, his own lips making contact with her right ear.

Her shudder told him what he needed to know. Not revulsion this time. Or even nerves. Excitement, pure and simple. Or not so pure, perhaps.

He purred seductively, 'I'm big and hard, Renée, and I'm hot. Very hot. Can't you feel me?' He pressed himself against the softness of her buttocks. 'See how much I want you? Don't you want me back, just a little?'

A cry escaped her lips as she spun round in his arms then glared up at him with the most telling colour in her cheeks. 'I *hate* you, Rico Mandretti,' she declared, even as her arms wound up around his neck and she lifted her parted lips towards his.

Rico heard her declaration, but actions spoke louder than words. And her actions told him she did want him. Maybe more than a little.

'I like your brand of hate,' he returned, and, sweeping his arms tightly around her, he crushed her body against his just as his mouth crashed down on hers.

His kiss was savage, but she didn't shrink from it. If anything, she met him more than halfway, taking his tongue avidly into her mouth, sucking on it, displaying a hunger every bit as wild and uncontrollable as his. He kissed her and kissed her, then kissed her some more till she was like dough in his arms and he himself was incoherent with desire and need. Finally, he dragged her down into the plush green pile and began pulling at her clothes.

Did she help him? Or was it all his doing? Whatever, they were both soon naked from the waist down and he was pushing her legs wide apart and touching her there, there where she was wet, oh, so wet. He groaned, then touched her some more, thrilling to the evidence of her arousal. She surely wouldn't be able to say afterwards that she hadn't wanted him. His fingers slipped easily inside her and she moaned, her head threshing from side to side on the carpet.

'No, no,' she began whimpering, but he knew she didn't mean for him to stop. She wanted him inside her, not his hands. And that was where he wanted to be too, despite knowing he was going way too fast. Where were all his supposed skills in the bedroom now? He wasn't going to be able to control himself much longer here. He had to have her. *Now!*

Within a heartbeat, he was pushing into her, filling her to the hilt. He gasped at the rush of wild elation which ricocheted through him. What delicious heat, what sweet surrender.

But the surrender was going to be all his. And soon.

Perhaps if her long, lovely legs weren't already wrapped tightly around him and she wasn't urging him on, her nails digging into his already tensed buttocks, he might have stood a chance of lasting. As it was...

'Oh, hell,' he muttered when his thighs and belly tightened and he knew from experience that he was about to come. Years of practising safe sex finally sent warning bells clanging through his bedazzled brain but it was already far too late.

They groaned together, then came together, fierce violent spasms worthy of five years of foreplay. His back arched, as did hers, and then he was clasping her to him, holding her tight as his seed pumped away inside her, recklessly refusing now to care about the consequences.

So what if he made a baby with her? It wouldn't be the end of the world. It might, in fact, Rico started thinking as his orgasm gradually began to fade away, be the beginning of a brave new world. For him. For her.

He'd always wanted children. And he'd always wanted Renée, from the first moment he'd set eyes on her.

She slipped her legs away from his waist with an exhausted sigh, her arms also abandoning his body to flop out by her sides. He levered his body weight up onto his elbows and stared down at her flushed face, which was tipped sideways, her eyes shut but her lips still apart. Her breathing was shallow, but slowing.

'Are you all right?' he asked softly.

Her head turned to face him and her eyes opened, as cool and calm as ever. 'You mean, am I lying here worrying myself sick because I've just had unsafe sex with a notorious playboy?'

Rico gritted his teeth. Nothing had changed. Once sarcastic, always sarcastic.

'I am not,' he ground out, 'and never have been a notorious playboy. But, that aside, let me assure you this is the first time I've had unsafe sex since leaving Jasmine. And before you ask, yes, I had myself cleared with blood tests once I realised what kind of creature *she* was. What about you?'

'You needn't worry, Rico,' she said with a weary sigh. 'About anything.'

'You mean you're protected against pregnancy?'

'Trust me when I say there will be no baby. What do you take me for?' she snapped. 'A complete fool?'

Rico gnashed his teeth. What kind of fool was *he* for even considering a future with this woman? What kind of wife would she make? Or mother, for that matter?

'What about everything else?' he persisted. After all, just because she hadn't been sleeping with Wade Jackman didn't mean she hadn't had other lovers. Obviously, she had a pretty high sex drive, the way she'd just carried on. She scorned him for being a playboy but that modelling world she moved in wasn't exactly renowned for being conservative in the sexual department. They were an incestuous lot from what he could see, a bit like the acting world.

'If you must know, this is the first time I've had unprotected sex in so long it doesn't matter. Given I'm a regular blood donor, I can guarantee I'm safe.'

'Well, aren't you a goody two-shoes?' he mocked.

'And aren't you glad that I am? Just think. A whole

month of condomless sex if you like. Now, that's a male fantasy these days, if ever there was one.'

Rico had to confess that the idea did appeal to him. A lot. He stirred at the thought of being able to have sex with her at any time without the worry or awkwardness of using protection, his response reminding him he was still inside her, his flesh encased snugly in hers. *More* snugly by the moment.

Her eyes flared wide. 'You can't be,' she said disbelievingly. 'Not this soon.'

'We playboys can just go and go,' he said with a superb poker-face. 'Or should that be come and come? Whatever, the result is the same. Very happy partners. But let's try it with the rest of your clothes off this time. I've always wanted to see you naked.'

Colour zoomed back into her cheeks, pleasing Rico no end. He liked seeing her rattled. He should have known, however, that she'd soon recover.

'You too, then,' she countermanded. 'I'm not going to be the only one in my birthday suit.'

'My pleasure,' he said, and whipped his top off in a flash.

There was no doubt she liked what she saw.

'I knew you'd have a lovely hairy chest,' she murmured as she slid her fingers slowly and sensuously through the centre of his hair-matted chest. Her eyes, which had been sharp and clear a moment before, clouded over and she appeared quickly lost in another world. Her focus was all on the dark curls which covered his chest then formed an arrow that ran downwards. When her fingers started following that arrow, his stomach sucked in sharply. But she only went as far as his navel before retracing her steps upwards. Any relief was short-lived, however, when she discovered his already hardened nipples and started playing with them. Rico gasped, then grabbed her wrists.

'No more of that,' he growled, 'or this will be over before it begins.' Hell, she turned him on quicker than any woman he'd ever been with. He was already fully erect again. Maybe hate was an aphrodisiac.

'Like the first time, you mean?' she scoffed.

'You were just as quick,' he reminded her. 'Now take off the rest of your clothes. But do it slowly. I want to watch.'

Her eyes flashed. 'You're a wicked devil, do you know that?'

'Just stop talking and get your gear off, mistress mine.'

She glared at him as she struggled out of the pale green cardigan, not an easy process when you were pinned to the floor. She had even more difficulty pulling the short-sleeved jumper up over her head and he had to help.

'I'm going to buy you some far more accessible clothes,' he muttered darkly. 'Either that, or I'll just keep you naked all the time you're with me.'

She stared up at him whilst he stared down at her bra.

It was made of pale pink satin, a nothing-thing not designed to enhance or exaggerate. He'd been right about her not being flat-chested. She wasn't nearly as busty as Jasmine, or Leanne, or a lot of the women he'd dated over the years, but what he was seeing through that pink satin looked nicely round and soft, with hard centres, the way he liked his chocolates.

Her hands went to the front-opening clasp before hesitating.

'Don't be shy,' he said thickly. 'You must know you're beautiful.'

'I…I always thought you preferred voluptuous women,' she said a bit shakily.

Her sudden lack of confidence touched him.

'And blondes!' she added more stroppily.

He smiled. 'I do. You're the exception. Here. Let me do it.' He brushed aside her reluctant hands and undid her bra, slowly peeling the cups back to reveal exquisitely shaped breasts with deliciously dark aureoles and large, fiercely erect nipples. Once he'd wriggled her right out of the garment and tossed it aside, he couldn't resist bending to suck them. She didn't stop him, arching her back at first contact, then cradling his head at each breast as if he were a much loved infant.

Rico found the experience incredibly sexy, yet at the same time amazingly comforting, like being wrapped in a big, warm towel after a long, hot bath. He could have stayed suckling on her breasts forever.

His hair suddenly being tugged upward brought a cry of shock from his lips. He lifted his head and frowned questioningly down at her flushed face.

'No more,' she said huskily. 'Or I'll come.'

He blinked. No kidding? From just doing that?

And then he felt it, her insides squeezing then releasing him, over and over. Her need for another orgasm, he realised, was acute.

'Just how long has it been since you've been with a man?' he asked her.

Her face twisted into a grimace almost like pain. 'Please don't start asking me stupid questions,' she choked out. 'At least a week, OK? Now, just do it, will you? Do it hard and fast.'

Once Rico had decided that her crack about a week had to be sarcasm, he fell to the task with gusto. Hard and fast she wanted it. Hard and fast was what she was going to get.

'Oh, God,' she groaned after several thrusts, which spurred him on to more vigorous efforts.

'God help me,' she cried and clasped him to her, inside and out.

God help me too, Rico thought. For how was this going to cure him of his sexual obsession for Renée Selinsky? He'd never been with a woman like her. So contradictory. So intriguing. So...exciting. All this would do, he feared, was make him want more. And more. And more.

But then he remembered he could have all he wanted of her for the next month. A month was quite a long time.

He just hoped it would be long enough...

CHAPTER SEVEN

RICO woke to silence, and no one in the bed with him. The empty champagne bottle was propped up on what had been her main pillow, a rolled-up sheet of notepaper funnelled into its neck.

Snatching it out, he unrolled the paper onto the crumpled sheets and read what she'd written.

Dear Don Juan,

it began.

Sorry I can't stay for breakfast, or afters. I have an appointment at André's in town at eight. If you know anything about the popularity of André's beauty salon, you'll understand why I refuse to cancel. Then I have some shopping to do afterwards before heading off to the races, as usual. I'm sure you'll find me there. You know my regular haunts. I presume you have something in mind for this evening, so, being a good little mistress, I'll arrange to be free.
 Ciao,
 Renée
 P.S. Don't shave!

Rico frowned down at the postscript. Don't shave. What did she mean by that? Was she being sarcastic again?

Hell, was she ever anything else?

Rico crushed the note in his hand, his mood instantly black. If ever a woman had the knack of spoiling things, it was her. They'd had a fabulous night together. More than fabulous, damn it! And what had she done? Run out on him the first chance she got!

Any other female would have still been here, in this bed, cuddled up to him and wanting more of what he had finally expertly delivered. He'd had her purring with pleasure for hours, and sighing with satisfaction over and over. The least she could have done was stay.

'But no!' Rico snarled as he brushed aside the curtains around the bed and climbed out, forgetting in his temper that the bed was on a stupid platform. His foot suddenly found air instead of carpet, his language extremely colourful as he slipped down the steps and crashed to the floor, not far from where he and Renée had first had sex.

Winded but not hurt, he lay there for a moment before glaring balefully up at the nearby statues.

As much as Renée had seemed startled by his ability to bounce back, she'd been very happy to take full advantage of his unabating desire for her. Very, very happy! No wonder she hadn't wanted him to reduce their bet to one night. She probably got off on the idea of having a lover like him on tap for a month, one who would bust his britches to satisfy her, and be prepared to pay for the privilege as well. The woman was wicked, he decided. Wicked and perverse and more lusty than any woman had a right to be!

Scrabbling up from the floor, he staggered into the black marble bathroom, only to be confronted with more evidence of their decadent evening together. Two empty champagne glasses sat beside the huge spa bath, which was still full of water, though the bubbles were long gone. The almost empty food platter was on the floor, alongside a pile of crumpled towels. Rico pulled the plug on the bath and picked up the platter before leaning on the vanity and peering into the mirror at his bleary, bloodshot eyes.

The memory of other eyes in that mirror immediately jumped into his mind. Green eyes, dilated with desire as their owner clung to the vanity-unit edge, staring wildly at him behind her whilst he did what she liked most, being taken that way.

The memory disturbed him. Because it wasn't what he *really* wanted, just being her stud. Yet that was what he'd reduced himself to last night, he realised. Him, just servicing her every which way. Him, trying to outdo himself each time.

No wonder she'd mockingly called him Don Juan. Clearly, that was all she thought he was good for. There'd been no meaningful conversation between them, nothing but provocative banter designed to keep their minds focused on sex and their bodies ready to accommodate their thoughts. In the end, he'd proved himself to be exactly what she'd always accused him of being. Shallow!

But not selfish, he conceded ruefully. She had to give him that. Her pleasure had been his first concern.

Or had it?

Had he pulled out all the stops *just* to satisfy her, or to *show* her how darned good he was in bed? What part had his male ego had to play in last night's many and varied performances?

A lot, he finally accepted and winced at the realisation.

'Oh, Rico, Rico, Rico,' he said, shaking his head

at the man in the mirror. 'What kind of man are you really? The essentially decent guy your mother thinks you are? Or the superficial, self-centred rake that Renée sees when she looks at you?'

Serious soul-searching was something Rico hadn't attempted in a good while. He'd been forced to have a partial look at himself a few months back when he'd jumped to hasty conclusions about Charles' wife and caused the poor devil no end of trouble. But all he'd discovered about himself at that time was that he'd become a cynic about beautiful women. With good cause, too.

There were a lot of mercenary females out there with their eye on the main chance, namely a rich husband.

Renée had once been one of them.

Not any more, apparently. She didn't seem even slightly interested in catching herself another Joseph Selinsky. Or a Rico Mandretti. Yet she must know she could if she wanted to.

It wouldn't take much to tip his lust for her into full-blown love. Hell, he only had to remember that moment when he'd thought she might have conceived to know his feelings for the woman ran deeper than desire.

Who knew why? It was truly perverse. And he was truly sick to death of thinking about her.

Clearly, she wanted to remain footloose and fancy-free. She wasn't remotely interested in remarrying or ever having a family. All she wanted from the men in her life was what he'd given her last night.

The *men* in her life?

Rico scowled, then spun on his heel and hurried out into the bedroom to where he'd thrown the crumpled note. Scooping it up from the carpet, he smoothed it out again and reread the part where she said she'd arrange to be free.

His whole insides contracted. Did that mean she would have to cancel a date tonight?

'At least a week,' she'd said to him when he'd asked her how long it had been since she'd had sex. He'd thought she was joking. With hindsight, he conceded that she might not have been. A woman with her obviously high sex drive probably had a hot date every Saturday night.

A black jealousy ripped through Rico at the thought of her doing the things she'd done with him last night with any other man. He couldn't change the past and obliterate her previous lovers, but he aimed to make sure she understood there would be *no* other men during the next month. Mistresses gave their lovers *exclusive* rights to their bodies.

At least, they were *supposed* to.

But mistresses didn't always do what they were supposed to do, Rico accepted. And neither would Renée. She would run her own race, make her own rules. He hadn't stipulated exclusiveness on that piece of paper. A bad mistake on his part.

He wouldn't mind betting she hadn't made any mistakes with her *written* demand.

It really annoyed him that she'd destroyed her darned wager. He'd like to have seen exactly how she'd worded her demand for his share of Ebony Fire. As he recalled, she hadn't taken long to write it down. He'd had more difficulty, both over the wording and the fact the Biro hadn't worked well because he had nothing underneath his sheet of paper except the felt-topped card table, whereas she had had the rest of the notepad for support.

A light suddenly went on in Rico's brain. The notepad! What Renée had written might still be visible on the notepad. He'd seen how detectives handled such things on television and in the movies. They rubbed a pencil softly over the next page sideways, making sure the carbon didn't sink into the indentations of the writing and, pronto, the words that had been written on the missing page were magically revealed!

Rico raced over and snatched up the phone and dialed Reception, where he gave his name then asked to be put through to the presidential suite. James answered, making Rico wonder if the man ever slept. Still, it was after nine. Not all that early.

'It's Mr Mandretti here, James,' he announced, trying not to sound as excited as he was feeling. 'I need to speak to Ali, if he's up.'

'His Highness is having his morning coffee out on the balcony. I will take the phone out to him.'

Ali eventually came on the line.

'Good morning, Enrico. To what do I owe the honour of your call?'

'I need to ask a favour.'

'Of course. If it is within my power to grant it.'

Rico rolled his eyes. Ali's formal way of speaking sometimes irritated him. But he was such a great guy otherwise that Rico tolerated his being slightly pompous.

'I need to come up and have a look at that notepad which we used to write our bets on last night,' he confessed. No point in trying to pull the wool over Ali's eyes. No need to, either. Ali would understand perfectly why he wanted to know what Renée had written.

'Come up from where? Oh. Oh, I see. You spent the night here in the hotel. I presume, then, that the lovely Mrs Selinsky did not stay the whole night with you?'

Rico shook his head from side to side. As he'd just been thinking. No point in trying to fool Ali.

'She had an early hairdressing appointment,' Rico replied. 'We're meeting up again at the races this afternoon.'

'Now, what is that saying? You don't let grass grow under your shoes?'

'Under my feet,' Rico corrected. 'And you're right. I don't. I've always lived by the motto of not putting off till tomorrow what you can do today.'

'Or last night,' Ali said, his tone drily amused.

'Exactly.'

'I won't be uncouth and ask you how things went. I will be able to judge for myself shortly. So yes, do come on up, my friend, and have coffee with me. I'll get James to locate the notepad and have it waiting. I presume you also want a pencil. Soft-leaded?'

'Yes, that'd be great. I knew I could count on your co-operation. And your understanding.'

The laughter down the line was deep and rich, a bit like Ali's bank accounts. 'We men have to stick together. Especially when the lady concerned is both beautiful *and* complicated.'

'You can say that again,' Rico muttered. 'I won't be a tick. I just need to put some clothes on.'

He could hear Ali chuckling as he hung up.

CHAPTER EIGHT

RICO rarely admired other men's looks. But as he walked out onto the balcony of the presidential suite, it was difficult not to notice that Ali lounging back in the morning sunshine in cream silk pyjama bottoms and nothing else was a sight to behold. If his Arab friend ever decided to become a movie star, then a remake of *The Sheikh* would be the perfect vehicle for him. Not totally surprising, since that was what he was. But not all real sheikhs looked like the Hollywood version.

Ali did. He had it all. The rich olive skin. Jet-black hair and eyes. High cheekbones and hawkish nose. A lean, well-honed body and a predator's mouth. Plus sufficient hair on his chest to be primitively sexy without being beast-like.

Rico could well understand why the ladies threw themselves at him. They were the same reasons women had thrown themselves at *him* over the years.

But looks were not the be-all and end-all, Rico had come to realise, more so lately than ever before. A man had to be more than the sum total of his inherited genes.

He wondered if Ali's good looks had been more hindrance than help to him in *his* life. One day, Rico would ask him. But not this morning. This morning, Rico had other things on his mind.

'Good morning, Enrico,' Ali said with a flashing smile which would not have gone astray on a Barbary

Coast pirate. Yet if you closed your eyes he sounded like an English aristocrat. A most unusual mix. 'You do look well, if a little frazzled. Sit down. Some coffee? Or do you want to uncover your lady's secret straight away?'

Rico sat down at the table and picked up the notepad that was lying there, waiting for him, along with a pencil.

'She's not my lady. Not really.'

Ali frowned. 'I'm not sure I understand. If she spent the night with you, then surely she—'

'That was part of my prize for winning the hand,' Rico broke in. He had decided to confess everything on the way up in the lift. He needed another man's opinion, and he couldn't talk to Charles about his situation with Renée. Charles would not have been sympathetic at all. Ali, on the other hand, lived his own life by less conventional rules than those society dictated, especially when it came to his relationships with the opposite sex, so surely he would not be quite so judgemental.

'I didn't ask for Renée to go out with me,' Rico went on. 'She lied about that. She was protecting Charles' sensitivities. I demanded she be my mistress. For a month. Starting last night.'

Ali's eyes showed more shock than Rico had anticipated.

'My friend,' Ali said carefully, 'I admire your boldness, but that is a dangerous game you're playing, especially with a woman like Renée.'

'I realise that now. That's why I have to see what she wrote; what *she* wanted from *me*.'

'What do you think she wanted from you?'

'My share of Ebony Fire. She loves that horse more than anything. She covets *all* of him.'

'As you coveted all of her.'

No point in denying it. 'Yes.'

'So you dangled your share of the horse as a carrot to tempt her to make that wager, knowing full well she would lose and have to become your whore.'

'My *mistress*,' Rico protested. 'Not my *whore*.'

'In my culture, it is the same thing. A mistress is a kept woman. She accepts money and gifts to make her body available for sex. That makes her a whore.'

Rico was beginning to think he'd made a mistake in confiding in Ali. It seemed he was more like Charles than he'd realised. 'We don't look at mistresses like that in the west,' he pointed out a tad irritably.

'I can't see how you can look at them any other way,' Ali countered. 'But, that aside, why are you so anxious to see what Renée asked for, when you already know?'

'I now think she might have asked for something else.'

'Why? Because she melted in your arms?'

Rico laughed. 'I wouldn't say melted, exactly. But she didn't object.'

'Such modesty, my friend. I'm quite sure she melted. You have a reputation for being…shall we say…more than adequate in the bedroom?'

Rico stiffened in his chair. 'Where in God's name would you hear something like that?'

'Without being indiscreet, I have to inform you that we shared a certain lady during the past year.'

'My God, who? Oh, of course. Silly of me not to guess. Leanne.'

'There is no need for us to exchange names, or notes. We are gentlemen, are we not? Let me just say that this certain lady raved about your—er—technique. But being a man as well as a gentleman, I was forced to demonstrate at length that Arab men of good breeding and culture are *never* surpassed in the bedroom.'

Rico could not help but be amused. So he'd been right in the first place. Ali was more pirate than gentleman. And a competitive, arrogant pirate at that. 'Just as long as we haven't shared Renée,' he said warningly.

'Only an Italian would be fool enough to take on a woman such as your merry widow,' Ali said quite seriously. 'Now, pick up the pencil and satisfy your curiosity. *And* mine.'

Rico wished his hand had been steadier. He didn't want to look more of a fool in Ali's eyes than he already did.

'Well?' Ali prompted when Rico finished and just stared down at the piece of paper. 'What does it say?'

Rico remained speechless. With a bewildered shake of his head, he handed the revealed note over to Ali. 'It doesn't make sense. It's crazy.'

'"*Marry me,*"' Ali read aloud, then glanced up, his own face puzzled. 'If you had asked her to marry you, then I would not have been surprised. But this…this is indeed a strange request from a woman who has done nothing but argue with you for the past five years.'

'You can say that again.'

'Could she possibly be secretly in love with you?' Ali asked.

'You *have* to be joking! She can't stand a bar of me. You know that.'

'No. I do not know that. What women say and what they *feel* are two entirely different things.'

'Renée does not love me,' Rico stated quite firmly. 'Trust me on that.'

'She *is* attracted to you, though, isn't she?'

Was she? Or was she attracted to and turned on by any good-looking guy who knew what he was doing in bed? 'She likes my looks and, yes, my technique, to coin your phrase. That's all. She told me last Sunday how much she dislikes me. And last night, she added that she now hates me.'

'Whereas you are madly in love with her.'

'What? No, no, I'm not. Definitely not. Why on earth do you say that? Or think it?'

'I've seen the way you look at her when she doesn't know you're looking at her. I know that look. It's the way I looked at a woman once. I recognise the symptoms of the disease. And it is a disease, being in love like that. It possesses and obsesses you. You can think of nothing else but being with her. You will do anything, risk anything, even your honour, to lie with her, even if it's just the once.'

Rico was taken aback by this unexpected confession. At the same time he was totally in tune with the emotions expressed. Ali understood. He'd been there, done that. But Rico still did not agree with him that he was truly in love with Renée. He wasn't madly in love at all. Just madly in lust.

'Who *was* she?' Rico asked.

Ali smiled the saddest smile. 'The one woman I could never have. My eldest brother's wife-to-be. The crown prince's betrothed.'

'Hell, Ali, that was rotten luck. So what happened?'

'What happened? Nothing happened,' he bit out. 'I was exiled here to Australia, my brother married my beloved, and their marriage remains a brilliant success to this day. They even have a handsome son and heir to prove it.'

The bitterness in his words and the abject bleakness in his eyes filled Rico's heart with pity for this man whom the world would perceive as having everything. Everything but the woman he loved. No wonder he never wanted to marry or have children. No wonder he had never fallen in love with any of myriad women he'd bedded since coming to Australia. His heart remained in Dubar, that was why. Either that, or it had been irretrievably broken.

'So why do you think Renée asked you to marry her?' Ali resumed, his eyes and his attention returning to the piece of paper he was holding. 'If not love, then what? Money?'

'That doesn't make sense, either. She's a very wealthy woman already. If she wanted to marry me for my money, she hasn't gone about achieving that end with any intelligence. You know how she acts around me. No, now that I've had time to think about, it's more likely to be spite.'

'Spite!' Ali repeated with surprise in his voice. 'I can't imagine many women marrying for spite. Still, Renée is not your usual woman. She runs very deep, that one.'

'Tell me about it. I can't work her out at all.'

Rico could work out the spite part, however. He remembered how she knew last night that he would demand sex as his prize. Had she decided to go one better, ask him for the one thing which she thought he would never want to give her? A wedding ring? Had it been a spur-of-the-moment burst of vengeance, something she had instantly regretted?

That certainly fitted the facts. And the woman. Rico recalled how he thought he'd detected relief in her when she hadn't won. She might have become afraid that he would relish marrying her, just to spite *her*.

'Going back to the motive of money,' Ali said, interrupting Rico's train of thought, 'I wouldn't dismiss that motivation out of hand. Renée might not be as wealthy as we presume. She might have had some bad luck on the stock market. There have been some mammoth losses recently, both locally and overseas. Also, her own business might not be going well. Remember, she lives high and likes to gamble. Maybe she's frittered a lot of her dead husband's money away. It might be worthwhile for you to find out the exact state of her finances.'

Whilst Rico believed he'd already worked out the reasons behind Renée's surprising demand, he conceded that Ali did have a point. It was worth checking out. No way would he want to risk ever falling into the hands of another devious fortune-hunter.

'I agree with you wholeheartedly. But how am I going to do that? I can hardly ask to look at her bank statements.'

'Use that detective agency you hired to check up on Charles' wife,' Ali suggested, leaning forward to refill his coffee-cup from the pot. 'They'll be able to do it quite easily. They have the right contacts and the right computer equipment. They can find out things which ordinary people can't.'

Rico's first reaction to this suggestion was negative in the extreme. Renée had gone right off her brain when she found out he'd had Dominique investigated. If she ever discovered he'd done the same to her, she would…

What? Rico asked himself irritably. What would she do? Hate him some more? She already hated him.

Besides, there were things other than her financial status which he would like to know. Like how many other men she had slept with since her husband died? And who?

'There is another reason which brings women to the altar,' Ali said. 'Could she possibly want a baby?'

Rico stopped breathing. A baby…

'The woman is thirty-five years old,' Ali went on. 'She doesn't have too many more child-bearing years ahead of her. You are always saying you want a family. And, despite what Renée has said to you in the past, we all know you would make a good father and possibly even a good husband. You're Italian, after all,' he said with an engagingly warm smile. 'Maybe that's her secret heart's desire. To have a child.'

Rico swallowed. Could Ali be right? And if he was, could Renée still be intent on securing her heart's desire, *without* the wedding ring?

A month of condomless sex, she'd promised him. But what if her reassurances over her being safe had all been lies? What if a baby *was* her secret heart's desire?

If so, what else had she lied about last night? Or faked?

No, no, he couldn't accept that reasoning. Renée's responses to him had not been pretence. She'd enjoyed the sex. *All* of it. No woman who was faking orgasms went that far.

No, a baby was not what she wanted from him,

Rico decided, despite not *wanting* to come to that conclusion. The idea had excited him momentarily, as it had last night. But it was a false and futile excitement, born of a desperate desire to believe his relationship with Renée could become more than a one-month forced affair. Renée would never choose him as the father of her baby, if a baby was what she wanted. Frankly, he'd be the last man on this planet she would choose.

No, *spite* was the odds-on favourite reason for her asking him to marry her. Money was the second favourite, although still a rank outsider. But worth looking into. Leopards didn't change their spots. She'd married once for money. If her chips were down, she'd do it again. She might not be broke as such, but women like Renée had one credo in life. You could never be too rich, or too thin. Just as Ali said, she was a high-maintenance gal.

'You're right,' Rico said. 'I'll have her finances investigated.' Amongst other things. He was curious to see just who she *had* been sleeping with since her husband died. And how many.

Meanwhile…

He ripped off the top sheet of the notepad and stood up. 'You won't mind if I keep this, will you?' he said as he slipped it into his trouser pocket.

'What are you going to do with it?'

'Nothing. Yet. But it seems silly to destroy evidence.'

'Why don't you just tell her you love her and ask her to marry you?'

Rico stared down at Ali then burst out laughing. 'Would you, if you were in my shoes?'

'If I were in your shoes, I would have made marriage my prize in the first place, not just sex. Then I would have had both.'

Rico laughed again. 'I see you've not become fully acquainted yet with the ways of the western world. Marriage in this country does not give a man automatic rights to his wife's body.'

Ali looked truly taken aback. 'Then why marry?'

'Exactly. You might have noticed that more and more Australian men are not exactly rushing off to the altar.'

Ali shook his head. 'A sad state of affairs if a man can't make love to his wife when he wants to. I would not enter into that kind of marriage. Was that a problem with your first wife?'

'No.'

'No, I didn't think so. A piece of advice, then, my friend. If you find money is not the issue here and you still want Renée as your wife and not just your mistress, why don't *you* try to get her pregnant? Women can change their attitude to a man once a baby comes into the picture,' he added with a touch of irony, Rico imagined.

'That's a thought, but I don't have control of the contraception part. She's on the Pill. And yes, I know if you were in my shoes you'd probably kidnap the object of your desire and whisk her off to some remote hideaway where there was no Pill and nothing to do but make your beautiful captive pregnant.'

God, but that *was* a good idea. He'd be tempted if Renée wouldn't eventually have him arrested for kidnapping and rape and goodness knew what else.

Ali smiled. 'I might have done something like that once. But not now. Now I content myself with passing pleasures when it comes to the ladies. I suggest you do the same with the merry widow. Enjoy her for the next month, then be done with her.'

'This could mean the end of our Friday-night poker games,' Rico pointed out.

Ali shrugged his broad brown shoulders. 'All good things come to an end, my friend. But let's cross that bridge when we come to it. A good philosophy for life, don't you think?'

CHAPTER NINE

ACTUALLY, Rico did not agree. He liked to anticipate any upcoming bridges. He was a planner as well as a doer. He could never just sit back and not worry about future difficulties, if he thought he could change or solve them in advance in some way.

Which was why his first job after checking out of the hotel and walking back to his new city address was to contact IAS and give them the job of finding out Renée's present financial status, along with a full report on her private life over the past five years. He needed to know what he was dealing with here. And asking Renée for the information herself was not an option. She would not tell him the truth. On the contrary, he could guarantee that she would lie her spiteful little tongue out.

The boss of the investigation agency—his name was Keith—told Rico over the phone that he could expect to know the lady's financial status within the week, but it would take another couple of weeks before they could fully report on the other matter.

'Such enquiries take time, Mr Mandretti,' the man informed Rico. 'Especially since you said it was vital Mrs Selinsky not find out people were asking personal questions about her.'

Rico finally hung up, satisfied that he was at last using his brains where Renée was concerned. Amazing what a little distance could achieve. Ali was wrong about his being madly in love with the woman.

The disease he was suffering from was strictly sexual in nature. So far. Hopefully, he would be cured before it changed into anything else.

Meanwhile, he had to protect himself from any weird and wonderful agenda Renée might still have where he was concerned. Her demanding marriage on that piece of paper had really thrown him for a loop there for a while. She must have been momentarily out of her mind. He hoped so, anyway.

With a dry laugh he padded across his main living room and clicked open the sliding glass door which led out onto the wide, sun-bathed terrace which ran around three sides of the penthouse. Stepping out onto the terracotta-tiled floor, he walked over to lean against the tubular steel railing which framed the shatter-proof glass panels beneath.

Rico had always liked this place, inside and out. Its central location, along with its heated lap-pool and the spectacular views, put this particular penthouse in a class of its own. There weren't many apartments, even right on the harbour, where you could see so many Sydney icons from so many vantage points. The opera house. The bridge. Circular Quay. The Rocks. And, of course, the city itself.

Rico was admiring it all when the sun suddenly went behind a heavy bank of cloud, casting an instant gloom over the buildings and water below. When a cool breeze started ruffling his hair he turned and went back inside.

Shaking his head once more at the fickleness of Sydney's spring weather, he made his way over to the kitchen and set about cooking himself a belated breakfast. Food had been the last thing on his mind lately, his body and his brain having other priorities.

But, now that he thought about it, he was damned hungry. Clearly, his energy stores had been severely depleted by last night's activities. He would need to refuel if he was going to keep up with Renée tonight. He had to give the witch credit for one thing: when she honoured a bet, she sure as hell honoured it!

In no time, Rico had a king's breakfast in front of him and fresh coffee perking away, filling the air with its mouth-watering aroma. He settled himself at the breakfast bar and tucked in to a calorie-laden plateful of bacon and eggs, mushrooms, grilled tomato and French toast.

'Great kitchen, this,' he muttered to himself between mouthfuls.

With the preparation of food having become so much of his life, Rico was very appreciative of a good kitchen. This one was state-of-the art, with sleek white cupboards, black granite benchtops and the latest in stainless-steel appliances. It was also a pleasure to cook in. Very well designed in a U-shape, with an internal island and this very handy breakfast bar along one side, complete with comfy stools.

Actually, no, it hadn't come complete with these stools. Charles had taken all his furniture with him to his new home in Clifton Gardens. *He'd* been responsible for the purchase of these stools, which were very modern, in keeping with the kitchen. Steel-framed, with red leather seats.

They also matched the new dining and lounge suites he'd bought, along with the rest of the furniture, although he hadn't personally chosen a single thing. He'd commissioned a small but well-recommended interior-design company to do the job for him, telling the lady boss the style of furniture he liked—clean

lines and modern Italian. Plus the colours he liked—
primary. And presto, three weeks later he'd walked
right in to a totally user-friendly home.

The designer had taken care of everything. Linen,
crockery, cutlery, glassware as well. All stylish and
classy. She'd even had the kitchen cupboard stocked
with food. Rico had been impressed, and very
pleased.

He'd been renting a furnished apartment since his
divorce and hadn't owned a single household item.
Jasmine had been awarded everything of that nature,
claiming those things had meant more to her—the
little housewife at home—than him.

What a laugh. Jasmine hadn't even been able to
cook. He'd done all the cooking—when they'd stayed
home for meals, that was—and the cleaning service
that came in every morning had done everything else.

Looking back, Rico had to agree that he'd been a
short-sighted fool to marry Jasmine. He'd been se-
duced by his ego—and other parts of him—into thinking she loved him, and vice versa. He should have
known that if he'd truly loved her, he would never
have been so attracted to Renée.

Renée…

Back to her again. He had that woman on his brain.
Well, at least he *had* done something about the situation with her. Not that his mistress-for-a-month solution would necessarily solve anything. He had an
awful suspicion that come the end of the month, his
sexual obsession with Renée would have grown, not
dissipated.

Don't shave.

The provocative P.S. on her note this morning

NO POSTAGE
NECESSARY
IF MAILED
IN THE
UNITED STATES

BUSINESS REPLY MAIL
FIRST-CLASS MAIL   PERMIT NO. 717-003   BUFFALO, NY

POSTAGE WILL BE PAID BY ADDRESSEE

HARLEQUIN READER SERVICE
3010 WALDEN AVE
PO BOX 1867
BUFFALO NY 14240-9952

Get FREE BOOKS and a FREE GIFT when you play the...

LAS VEGAS
GAME

Just scratch off the gold box with a coin. Then check below to see the gifts you get!

YES! I have scratched off the gold Box. Please send me my **2 FREE BOOKS** and **gift for which I qualify.** I understand that I am under no obligation to purchase any books as explained on the back of this card.

▼ DETACH AND MAIL CARD TODAY! ▼

306 HDL DUYK   106 HDL DUYZ

FIRST NAME

LAST NAME

ADDRESS

APT.#

CITY

STATE/PROV.

ZIP/POSTAL CODE

(H-P-03/03)

Visit us online at www.eHarlequin.com

7	**7**	**7**	Worth TWO FREE BOOKS plus a BONUS Mystery Gift!
🍒	🍒	🍒	Worth TWO FREE BOOKS!
🔔	🔔	♣	TRY AGAIN!

jumped into his mind, and he reached up to rub the stubble on his chin.

Impossible to put anything but a sexual connotation on that request. Impossible not to start wondering what erotic fantasy had inspired it. Over which erogenous zone did she want him to rub his hair-roughened skin? The same places he'd poured champagne over last night, then licked it off?

His stomach crunched down hard at the images that sprang into his mind. Last night had turned out very differently from what he'd anticipated. There'd been no need to seduce her—not after those initial few moments. She'd been with him all the way. And then some.

There'd been times when she'd astounded him with her passion, and her need. She simply couldn't get enough of him.

That was why he'd been so put-out when he woke this morning to find she was gone. Because he'd begun to believe—or hope—that it was him personally that she wanted and needed. Clearly, that wasn't the case. Clearly, she was simply a highly sexed creature who'd possibly gone too long without a man. He would be very interested to find out exactly how long it had been since her last lover.

Rico suddenly realised he'd been sitting there for ages without eating. When he tried another mouthful, he grimaced before reluctantly swallowing. Everything was stone-cold. Oh, well, at least he'd finished most of it. And there was still the coffee.

Getting up, he walked round to the sink and scraped the rest of the food down the disposal unit, then put all the utensils tidily into the dishwasher before pouring himself a corpse-reviving mug of very strong coffee. After he added a hefty slurp of milk and three teaspoonfuls of sugar he set off for the master bedroom, sipping as he went.

Time was slipping away and he didn't want to be late for the races. He didn't want to miss a second of being in Renée's stimulating company.

As it turned out, however, Rico *was* late for the races. He'd forgotten that they were not on at Randwick that Saturday afternoon, but at Rosehill Gardens, which was on the opposite side of the city. He'd almost reached Randwick and had just turned on the car radio to the racing channel when an announcement made him realise his mistake. Cursing, he swung the Ferrari into a U-turn and headed west. But by the time he arrived and parked his car, the first race was already under way. He could hear the cheering as he hurried across the car park.

'Damn and blast,' he muttered frustratedly to himself.

Once inside the members' enclosure he headed straight for the members' stand and the bar where Renée was most likely to appear between races. A drink was called for by then, something long and cold. A beer. Not that the weather was hot, or even warm. That cloud earlier had thickened and the day was overcast and cool.

Not so Rico. He felt as if he had a furnace stoking up inside him.

By the time he'd finished his beer there was still no sign of Renée, so he wandered out onto the veranda, which overlooked the grounds below, his gaze scanning the groups of people still standing around on the expanses of lawn or leaning against the saddling-enclosure fence. The horses had by then returned from the track, with the jockeys dismounting to go inside to be weighed. The four place-getters were standing in their parallel-placed stalls, steam rising from their flanks. The winner's trainer was beaming and the happy owners—a large group of middle-aged suits—were chatting and laughing together.

Rico envied them for a moment. There was nothing like leading in a winner. But then his eye was caught by a sight that drove all thought of winning races from his mind.

Renée was standing on the lawn, chatting away with some strange man. But not the Renée Rico was used to seeing at the races. Not the one who always wore a tailored trouser suit in some bland colour, along with sensible pumps, little make-up and a simple, smooth hairstyle. This Renée was totally different.

She was wearing a dress for starters, a smart black wrap-around coat-style dress with padded shoulders, deeply cut lapels and a black leather cummerbund belt that pulled her already tiny waist into a double handspan size. The end result was an hourglass shape that drew the eye, first to the amazing amount of cleavage she had on display, and second to her legs, those gorgeous long legs that had been wrapped so deliciously tightly around him last night.

Usually, she kept them hidden under trousers. Today they were encased in shimmering black pantihose and easily admired, courtesy of the shortness of her hem and the height of the killer shoes she was wearing. Black too, of course, with tall heels, pointy toes, cut-out sides and ankle straps. Quite wide, they were, as was the black satin ribbon she wore around her throat.

Rico could hardly believe his eyes. And the changes did not stop there. Her hair was different as well, both in colour and style. Jet-black now instead of walnut-brown. Still shoulder-length but layered and feathered around her face, as was the current fashion.

Rico couldn't say that it didn't suit her, because it did, as did her more extravagant eye-make-up and the scarlet gloss that shone brightly on her mouth, that mouth which had kissed him all over last night and which was at this very moment talking and laughing with another man, a rich-looking grey-haired gentleman, whose eyes were glued to her cleavage. Rico was less than fifty feet away so he knew damned well where that dirty old man was looking, and what he was thinking.

Had she sensed him standing up there at the railing, glowering down at her? Must have, for she lifted her face and their eyes connected, his instantly dark and dangerously jealous, hers sassy and sparkling.

She waved up at him before saying goodbye to her companion and heading towards the flight of steps that led up to where Rico was still standing, fists curled tightly over the railing. He remained right where he was, struggling to regain his composure, knowing full well that her appearance today was designed to torment him, not please him. She'd lost the bet last night but was still trying to win the war between them. How better to beat him than to turn him into a jealous, gibbering idiot as well as a bewitched, besotted fool.

She was the one intent on doing the seducing and the corrupting, he realised with sudden insight. That was what last night was all about, and what today was all about.

Rico's breathing quickened at the boldness of her counter-attack. He had to admire her. She had guts all right. And spirit. But it was a dampening thought that she *might* have faked a few things last night. Maybe she wasn't as enamoured of his technique as he'd imagined.

Whatever, he simply *had* to take her vamp-like appearance in his stride this afternoon or fall right into her trap. He thought he had himself under control again, but, as he turned to watch her join him on the veranda, her right knee lifted to take the final step and that action, combined with a puff of wind, flapped back the wrap-around slit in her skirt, giving him a gut-churning glimpse, not of pantihose but of lace-topped stockings and black suspenders, sensuously stretched against her soft, pale thighs.

The effect was instantaneous, and mortifying, Rico's only consolation being the fact he was wearing one of his more casual and loosely fitted black suits. Still, he moved swiftly to button up the jacket and hide his humiliation. To have Renée see the state she'd reduced him to so easily would have been the last straw. But it underlined to Rico that his imagining that a mere month would cure him of his desire for the merry widow was laughable.

Be damned, however, if he would ever give her an inkling of how he really felt. She wanted to tease and torment him? Play erotic games with him? Fine. He would wallow in every perversely pleasurable moment in private, then leave for Italy the moment the month was up, before she could deliver her *coup de grâce*, which of course would be to cut him dead.

One moment she'd be taking him to hedonistic heaven. And the next? Nothing. Zilch. Zero.

He wasn't sticking around for another five years of hell. No way. He would be out of her reach like a shot.

Not today, however. Today, she was all his. And he meant to take full advantage of the fact. He would play the game her way. But at the same time, *his* way. She wasn't going to get the better of him yet.

'My goodness, Renée,' he said silkily as she sashayed towards him with that lethal weapon of a skirt still flapping slightly open. 'When you take on a role you really like to get into the part, don't you? That outfit has sex-kitten mistress written over it, with just enough dominatrix built in to be tantalising. But don't you think you might have gone a little too far? Surely you don't want *every* old geezer you meet here today thinking you could be his, at a price. Or do you?' he went on before she could draw breath and reply. 'Maybe you've always been a little whore at heart.'

It was a low blow, inspired perhaps by some spite of his own. But she didn't seem to mind. She just laughed.

'I think you could be right, lover. How else do you explain my enjoying being with *you* last night?'

Aah. So she *did* mind. Her sarcasm gave her away. Yet for some reason he wasn't offended this time. Perhaps he'd moved beyond that, now that he'd held her in his arms and made love to her, and, yes, watched her come. Thinking back, he was pretty sure her many orgasms couldn't have all been faked. Perhaps her sarcasm was now a mocking not so much of him but of herself.

'Once I accepted I had this undeniable penchant

for bad boys,' she continued blithely, 'I decided to go with the flow, so to speak. Have some fun instead of resenting the situation. So when I left you this morning I thought, what the heck, Renée? Go for broke. I'd seen this little number last week in a boutique window and you said you wanted me to wear accessible clothes. Well, you don't get much more accessible than this, I can assure you.'

She leant close enough for him to get a more direct eyeful of cleavage and a noseful of her musky perfume.

And then she leant even closer.

'Are you game to see just how accessible, darling?' she murmured as her lips pressed against his cheek. 'We could find a relatively private corner somewhere here, I suppose. Or do you want to wait till tonight, when we're both climbing the walls?' Her lips moved over to brush his earlobe before she stepped back and eyed his quickened breathing with satisfaction. 'Or maybe you're climbing them already,' she added, and ever so gently pressed her hand between them, right over his straining erection.

He smiled. He had to, or scream. 'Now, now, Renée...' He took her hand equally gently and dropped it back by her side. 'Have some decorum. And please...don't forget who's the master here, and who's the mistress. I make the rules, not you. Which reminds me, how much do I owe you for this quite astonishing make-over?'

She shrugged, the movement momentarily lifting her already pushed-up breasts to more provocative heights. 'Not a cent,' she said. 'I'm a very cheap mistress.'

'*You* said that. *I* didn't. By the way, who was that gentleman you were just talking to?'

'An old friend of my husband's. Why?'

'He couldn't take his eyes off you.'

'I know.'

'You *like* old men ogling you?' he asked, his tone far too sharp.

'I like *you* ogling me,' she returned huskily.

His breath caught before he could stop it. Their eyes met, and this time, neither of them said a word. But it shimmered between them. The heat. The need.

A male hand clamping over his shoulder interrupted the sexually charged moment. 'Rico! Well, fancy running into you! Long time, no see. But aren't *you* doing well these days?'

Rice had turned to find that it was a man he'd worked with years ago in television. For a second he couldn't even remember his name. And then it came to him. Davidson. Ian Davidson.

'Not too bad, Ian,' he replied. 'And you?'

'Can't complain. I'm into wildlife documentaries now. They're always popular. A bit like cooking shows.'

'True.' Rico knew he should introduce Renée but he just didn't want to. He was already tired of the way men were looking at her today. Ian was no exception. He wasn't some old codger, either. He was relatively young, reasonably attractive, and his eyes were all over her.

'I heard you'd got divorced,' Ian said with another glance Renée's way.

'Yep,' was his abrupt reply.

'Aren't you going to introduce me to your lovely lady-friend?'

'No,' he replied curtly. 'I don't think I am.'

Renée rolled her eyes at him, hoisted the long strap of her black bag over her left shoulder and extended her right hand towards the still admiring Ian.

'I'm Renée,' she said.

Rico clenched his teeth when Ian eagerly shook the outstretched hand, then held it far too long.

'Renée,' Ian repeated, a smirk on his mouth. 'So, Renée, are you and Rico an item? Or just good friends?'

'Actually, I'm Mr Mandretti's mistress,' she said, perfectly poker-faced.

Rico couldn't help it. He laughed. Both at her gall and at Ian's sharply indrawn breath.

'Renée, darling,' Rico said, 'how naughty of you. She's not really my mistress, Ian. I just won her in a bet.' Two could play at being outrageous, his eyes told her. And Ian meant nothing to him. He could think what he liked.

Ian looked both perplexed and intrigued. 'Er—am I in the middle of some kind of game here?'

'I'm afraid you are,' Rico said. 'Renée is partial to games. And to gambling.'

'Now, that's the pot calling the kettle black,' Renée countered, green eyes glittering. 'Rico's the compulsive gambler here, Ian. But he's grown bored with betting for money. So he's upped the stakes to sex and sin. Next thing you know, he'll be wanting to play strip-Jack-naked with me right here in the stand.'

'Er—sounds fascinating, folks, but you'll have to excuse me for a moment. I happen to still like betting for money and there's a horse I want to bet on in the next race.'

'Good luck!' Renée trilled after him as he hurried off.

'You too, honey,' he called back over his shoulder with one last leer at her chest. 'Don't go away, now. I'll be back!'

Rico decided then and there that he could not tolerate any more of this type of banter—or encounter—this afternoon. Not in public, anyway. None of their horses were running today. There was no compelling reason for them to stay. But there were compelling reasons to go. Aside from his almost crippling need to make love to Renée again—and very, very soon—the thought of running into Ali with Renée dressed up like some expensive tart did not sit well on Rico. He really didn't want to have to smack his Arab friend right in his royal mouth, but he might if Ali started talking about whores again. *He* was the only one who could call Renée a whore, because he didn't really mean it.

'I don't want to play strip-Jack-naked,' he growled after Ian's departure. 'I want to play strip *Renée* naked. But not here in the stand. We're off to my place. Now.' When he took her arm in a firm grip, her eyes flashed green fire at him.

'And if I said no?' she snapped, the old Renée surfacing once more.

His fingers tightened as his eyes gleamed with dark resolve. 'I'd kiss you right here and now till you said yes.'

Was that a flicker of alarm that skittered through her eyes? If it was, it was gone in a flash.

'You would too, wouldn't you, you wicked devil?'

she said, but she was smiling. The new, go-with-the-flow, determined-to-have-fun Renée was back.

'You can count on it.'

She laughed. 'OK, so you've won this little skirmish. But the war is not over yet. Not by a long shot!'

CHAPTER TEN

'So WHERE have you parked *your* car?' Rico asked as he guided Renée swiftly through the open-air car park towards his Ferrari. Rico having been late for the races, his car was not exactly close.

'I didn't bring my car,' she confessed breathlessly. She was having some difficulty in keeping up in those ridiculous shoes. 'I came in a taxi.'

'Why's that?'

'It seemed silly to bring my car when I knew you would be taking me home after the races.'

'Aah. A girl who plans ahead. I like that.'

'Oh, I always plan ahead.'

I don't doubt it, Rico thought cynically, but didn't say so. They'd reached his car and he didn't want to start an argument.

'I expect you to stay with me for the rest of the weekend,' he told her as he helped her into the passenger seat.

She jerked her head up to stare at him, and again that odd moment of panic flashed into her eyes. But it was gone as quickly as it had come. 'In that case, I'll need you to take me home first.'

'Why's that?'

'I'll want a change of clothes. And some nightwear.'

He closed the passenger door and walked round to climb in behind the wheel before he looked at her again.

'You won't be needing any nightwear,' he said firmly, his eyes brooking no opposition.

Her blush astounded him.

He wanted to kiss her at that moment, but he knew if he did he would not be able to stop. And the front of a Ferrari was no place for lovemaking at all, let alone the kind he had in mind.

'Unless, of course,' he added, hoping to break the tension of the moment with some humour, 'you own a clinging black satin nightie with no back, even less front, and straps that refuse to stay on your shoulders.'

His goal was achieved because she laughed, her eyes sparkling with return mischief. 'No, but I do own a black satin corset, which has a built-in half-cup push-up bra and is so high-cut I had to have a full wax this morning before I could wear it today.'

Rico groaned and tried not to picture how she would look when he peeled that dress off her.

'I also have some red chiffon baby-doll pyjamas which you can see right through and which I've lost the panties to.'

'Stop!' he protested, then grinned and shook his head. 'And you called *me* a wicked devil.'

'I'm just being a good little mistress.'

'I think you're trying to make me fall in love with you,' he jested, then worried she might be doing just that.

Her startled expression showed he was way off-base.

'Then you'd be dead wrong, lover,' she confirmed.

'What about my money?' he asked, using the opportunity to pry a little. 'You interested in that?'

'Even less than I am in your falling in love with me. Look, we could go tit-for-tat here for ages, like we usually do. But, quite frankly, I'm sick and tired of all that. We've been acting like children around each other for far too long. If it makes you feel any better, I don't dislike and despise you as much as I thought I did. I'm sure you'll also be flattered to know that I've always found you disturbingly sexy. That's one of the reasons I used to have a go at you all the time. Because it bothered me how much I wanted you to f…'

She broke off and smiled a rueful little smile. 'Tch-tch. Have some decorum, Renée,' she lectured herself. 'Four-letter words are not really your style. I should have said it bothered me how much I wanted to sleep with you,' she amended sweetly.

Rico was more than flattered with this news. He was elated. But he did his best to remain cool and suave on the surface. 'I wish I'd known that. I thought I was the only one sitting there every Friday night in an agony of frustration.'

'Oh, no. I think I can safely say there were moments when I wanted to taking a running jump off that very high balcony.'

He grinned. 'I'm rather glad to hear that.'

'I don't doubt it. You're as egotistical as you are wicked. Oh, dear. I'm doing it again. Sparring with you.'

'Old habits do die hard.'

'Indeed. But honestly, Rico, let's not spoil the next month with silly spats and trying to get one over each other. Let's just enjoy each other for a change.'

'Sounds good to me. Like I told you once before, I'd rather make love than war.'

'Heavens, let's not go *that* far. What we're doing here is playing a game. And a pretty erotic game at that. But no more talk of love, please,' she swept on with a shudder. 'Or falling in love. I can't think of anything worse.'

Rico was taken aback, and tellingly hurt. But be damned if he was going to show it. 'That's an unusual thing for a woman to say,' he commented as he set about starting up the engine. Best to keep his expressive eyes away from her right at this moment. 'Love is usually the first thing a woman thinks of. And wants.'

'I'm an unusual woman,' she said offhandedly.

And a secretive one, Rico realised. Like Ali, she rarely revealed any details of a personal nature. This morning was the very first time his Arab friend had told him anything about his past, or his personal feelings. Renée was just as reticent.

'You know, Renée, I've known you for five years and I still have no idea what makes you tick.'

She presented him with one of those beautifully bland faces that she did so well. 'But you don't have to, Rico. Just concentrate on what you're going to do to me when you get me home. Mistresses aren't meant to be understood, just…used. Now there's an acceptable four-letter word. Used. You…*used*…me with incredible skill last night, Rico. Quite frankly, I've never had better.'

She possibly meant it as a compliment. But all Rico heard was his being compared with innumerable other lovers. On top of that, her mocking tone sounded both insulting and patronising. She was relegating him to the role of mindless stud again. A role he was beginning to have mixed feelings over. Because it wasn't enough.

Damn it! Had Ali and Charles both been right after

all? *Did* he love this woman? It didn't *feel* like love
when he looked at her. There were no warm, fuzzy
feelings in his stomach. Neither did he want to be
sweet or gentle with her. He wanted to ravish her.
And often. If that was love, then it was a darned pe-
culiar kind. Powerful, though. Darned powerful.

'Sounds like you've had a lot of experience,' he
couldn't resist commenting as he reversed out of the
car park.

She slanted him a dry look. 'I'm thirty-five years
old, Rico. I was a model for ten years, during which
time I had several boyfriends. I even lived with one
for a while. Added to that, I married an older man-
of-the-world type when I was in my late twenties, and
I've been a widow since I was thirty. So what do *you*
think?'

'I think I don't want to know,' he snapped. 'Just
tell me where you live. I *have* to know that if you
want me to take you there.'

She sighed, the sound echoing his own frustration
with the way they always ended up snapping and
snarling at each other, no matter what promises they
made.

'I have a town-house in Balmain.'

'Balmain,' he repeated, surprised. He thought a
woman with her money would have lived somewhere
more ritzy, like Double Bay, or on one of the northern
beaches.

Admittedly, Balmain had become a much more up-
market address than it had once been. All inner-
Sydney suburbs, even the ones in the west, now commanded top prices for their homes. Balmain had long
made the leap from working class to yuppie heaven,
with its elegant rows of trendily renovated terraces

and the opening of cafés and restaurants on every other corner.

'Don't you know where Balmain is?' she said, misinterpreting the surprise in his voice. 'I would have thought the *Passion for Pasta* king would be well acquainted with the place, since Balmain sports more Italian restaurants than Leichardt.'

'I know Balmain,' he said. 'I have friends there.'

'In that case, I won't need to give you directions till you get closer.'

'Fine,' he said, then fell broodingly silent. She did likewise, which was a relief to begin with, but then a torment. Their lack of conversation and his familiarity with the roads through western Sydney meant that his mind was left idle. The devil, it seemed, found just as much work for idle minds as idle hands. Rico soon started thinking about what he *was* going to do to her when he got her home, not the best train of thought when driving, as evidenced when he almost ran up the back of a truck.

'Keep your eyes on the road, will you?' Renée chided.

'My eyes *are* on the road,' he retorted. 'It's my mind that's gone AWOL. Look, Balmain's not far away. Start giving me directions.' Anything so that he stopped picturing her in that black satin corset and nothing else. Except the stockings and shoes, of course. He'd want her to keep those on as well for a while.

Geez, even getting road directions didn't do the trick!

Fifteen minutes later he sat outside her town-house in the car, tapping the steering wheel impatiently whilst she went in to collect what things she thought she needed.

'Don't be long,' had been his parting advice.

'I'll have to feed my goldfish,' she'd curtly informed him through the passenger-side window before whirling and wiggling her way across the pavement and up some steps onto a covered walkway that led into a small but exclusive-looking town-house complex.

He watched her disappear into the one furthest from the road. It was just like all the others. Cream brick, two-storeyed and quite stylish. But again, a lot less than a woman of her wealth could afford.

He'd be very interested in seeing that report on her financial status at the end of the week. But not so interested any more in seeing how many men she'd slept with during the past five years. She'd already admitted she'd been very sexually active. All that was left for Rico to find out, really, was with whom. Although he already had ideas on that. He'd bet London to a brick that they'd all be younger than her. Younger and easily dispensed with. Men she met through her work. Possibly male models or advertising executives or aspiring fashion photographers. The toy-boy type, as he'd thought before. It was clear Renée liked sex, but she liked it unencumbered with emotional involvement.

The thought riled him, as did the time she was taking in getting her damned things. If she was in there changing out of that black dress and black satin corset, he was going to strangle her.

Rico was just about to leap out and pummel on her front door when the lady herself made a reappearance, thankfully still in the same sexy gear, and carrying a reasonably large navy gym bag. Now he did leap out, meeting her before she reached the steps and sweeping the gym bag out of her hand.

'You're only staying for the weekend, Renée,' he said drily on feeling the weight of the bag. 'Not the whole month.' Though, having said it, Rico thought that wasn't a bad idea. But he knew she wouldn't go for that. He'd already pushed things, demanding she stay the weekend. Frankly, he'd been surprised when she'd agreed. Although of course her motivation was strictly selfish. She wanted more of what she'd waited so long for. More sex. More fun and games.

Come Monday morning, however, she'd be back to work. And so would he. He had a heavy schedule next week. Several episodes to shoot. Meetings with his accountant and solicitor about the restaurant franchises. And discussions with his television crew about the road-tour of Italy he was going to propose.

Oh, yes, that was definitely still on. Rico could already see the writing on the wall where Renée was concerned. He'd be out on his ear at the end of the month, no matter how well he performed in the bedroom. Except on the million chance she was after him for his money. If that was the case, then he certainly wouldn't be waiting around to become her next victim.

No. This month was all they were going to have together. Given that, he aimed to enjoy himself to the full. And to hell with silly worries about falling in love with her, or whatever other weird and wonderful agenda she had in mind.

Sex was the name of the main game. And it was a game he was eminently qualified to participate in. Same as the woman walking beside him.

Rico's gaze raked over that incredible black outfit again, putting his body right back on red alert for action.

'What in hell were you doing that took you so long in there?' he asked as he slung the bag into the boot. 'Besides packing the kitchen sink, that is.'

'I told you. I had to feed the goldfish.'

'How many have you got? Two thousand?'

She sighed. 'I went through the message bank on my phone as well. Made a few return calls.'

'Who to?'

'I don't think that's any of your business.'

'Fine,' he said through gritted teeth. 'Let's get going, then,' he added, resolving to shelve every thought about Renée for the next thirty-six hours except sexual ones. She wanted him in no other role except Don Juan? Fine by him. He could do that.

He started playing his part the second his front door was shut behind them and he'd disposed of her gym bag on the foyer floor, leaving his hands free to pounce. Her cry of protest when he pushed her up against the nearest wall failed to impress, as did her feeble attempt to shove her shoulder bag between them. That bag quickly joined the gym bag, leaving her with no weapons against him but her tongue. And *that*, he swiftly found after some serious French kissing, soon totally lost its usual caustic edge.

'You kiss very well,' she purred when he finally lifted his head.

'I do most things well,' he growled and stepped back just far enough to do what he'd been wanting to do since he first clapped eyes on her that day.

It was a struggle to keep his fingers from fumbling as he undid the leather tie that secured the cummerbund. But he managed, although his already pounding heart became even more erratic as he slowly unwound the darned thing. Her chest was rising and falling rapidly too, he noticed. Yet her face had grown quite pale, as if all the blood had run from her head.

'Don't you dare go fainting on me,' he warned just as the leather wrap ran out and slipped from her body, leaving the dress to hang more loosely around her but still secured in some way.

Press-studs, he soon found out.

He could have simply ripped the two sides of the dress apart, but he didn't want that. He wanted to torture her as much as himself. Her eyes had already grown wider and he could feel her tension, as well as her excitement. He knew how she was feeling, because he was feeling the same way, torn between the desire to draw out these exquisite moments of anticipation, and the urgent need to see everything at once, *do* everything with delay.

The knowledge that she wouldn't stop him doing anything he wanted at this stage gave him patience, and a wicked resolve to have her lose control first. Yes, to make her beg as he'd once vowed to make her beg. So he undid each press-stud slowly, taking his time, making sure his hands didn't brush against a single thing other than the soft black lightweight wool the dress was made out of. There was no accidental touching of exposed flesh, although he went darned close at times. She stood there silently and very stiffly, every muscle held exquisitely tight, both inside and out, he imagined.

At last every press-stud had yielded and he was peeling the dress back, back off her slender shoulders, giving up the secrets of what lay beneath.

His eyes didn't know where to wallow first, but inevitably they raked downwards.

Dear God. She hadn't lied about that corset being high-cut. There was nothing but the narrowest strip of black satin between her legs.

He wrenched his gaze upwards as he felt his own control beginning to slip. But the sight of her breasts pushed up and together in that decadently designed built-in bra did little to help. Every time she breathed in—which was often—her nipples tried to escape their confinement. He could already see a good proportion of each aureole.

There was no doubt the whole corset was a mastery of erotic engineering, boned to pull her waist right in, automatically making her hips flare out and her breasts look larger than they were. The choice of black satin was spot-on as well, the colour a perfect foil against her pale skin, the slick, shiny satin more feminine than leather but just as arousing. To him, at least. She could not have chosen better if she wanted to reduce him to mush.

A strictly emotional term, of course. His body was far from mush. It was like granite and screaming for release.

His eyes dropped downwards again, taking in her long, long legs and those devastatingly sexy suspenders. The screws on his own sexual tension tightened a notch. Truly, there was no safe place to look. Even if he closed his eyes, the memory of her in that outfit would stay with him.

'Wicked,' he murmured, then laughed. 'I don't even know where to start. Or what to do next. How many times have you done this to a man with this amazing outfit?'

'Never.'

'Huh?'

'I only bought it this morning. Like the dress. And the shoes. Everything…just for you, Rico,' she said thickly, her green eyes glazing over.

He couldn't decide if she was for real, or just playing with him. Maybe even lying to him.

If she was, he didn't want to know. Not right now. He reached out to smooth his hands down the sides of the corset, tracing the shape of her very feminine figure. When his hands spanned her tiny waist and squeezed, she gasped, quivering when he let her go. His hands continued their journey down the outside of her bare upper thighs then across the lace-topped stockings before starting up the inside towards the ultimate goal.

'Move your legs apart a little more,' he commanded, his voice sounding as if he were talking underwater.

'You…you can undo it,' she said shakily as she did what he wanted.

'Undo what?'

'Between my legs. There are snaps at the front and back. You can remove that part altogether.'

His eyes flicked up to hers then back to the task at hand. If his hands had fumbled before, they were all fingers and thumbs now. But it wasn't rocket science and the strip of satin which had so tantalisingly but inadequately covered her private parts was finally dispatched to the floor of the foyer.

He stepped back to view his handiwork, and to try to keep his brain working, even whilst his body was fast racing towards overload. She looked incredible. Stunningly sexy and beautifully bad. But not bad enough, he decided darkly, and reached out to tuck the bra-cups down against the undersides of her breasts, exposing all of her nipples. Already rock-hard, they were. And so eagerly awaiting his attention.

She gasped when he gave each a tweak before stepping back once more to see how she looked now.

'That's better,' he said, and took no notice whatsoever of the look in her eyes, or the way she was pressing her palms against the wall beside her as if she was some kind of virgin sacrifice, pinned to the wall against her will. What an actress!

This was *exactly* what she wanted, what she'd planned to happen all day, to torment and arouse him unbearably with her choice of clothes and underwear, firing an insatiable appetite in him so that he would, yes, use her as she wanted to be used.

'Like I said,' he muttered, 'wicked.'

'Rico, I—'

'Hush up,' he snapped. 'I like my mistresses silent. Except when they're begging, of course. Is that what you were going to do, Renée? Beg?'

Their eyes clashed. Slowly the panic left hers, replaced by a dark and bitter resolve which almost eclipsed his. But not quite. Rico in full-on fury mode was an unstoppable and unsurpassable force.

'I'd die before I'd beg anything from you,' she threw at him.

He smiled. 'We'll see, sweetheart. We'll see. Don't go away, now.'

He delighted in the anguish that immediately filled her face. 'Where...where are you going?' she choked out, levering herself away from the wall. Clearly her leaning position had been supporting her because, once away from the wall, she swayed dangerously on her heels.

'To my bedroom,' he informed her. 'To slip into something more…comfortable. Don't worry. I'll be back. But before I go…' he strode over and pressed her back hard against the wall, palms splayed wide as before '…perhaps a little taster of what's to come…'

He clasped her face with one hand and held it captive, watching her eyes whilst he touched her with his other hand, touched her there between her legs, where she was silky smooth but shockingly wet. Touched her inside and out. Touched her everywhere but right on that spot he knew would send her screaming into a climax. Touched her till her iron will broke and he saw an anguished pleading enter her eyes. It wasn't verbal begging but it was almost as good.

When a moan broke from her lips he let her go.

'I won't be long,' he said with a final patronising peck on her panting mouth.

'You bastard,' she spat. 'If you think I'm going to stay here and wait for you to come back like a good little girl, then you can think again.'

'You *will* stay. Or I won't *be* back. I'll walk out of here right now. There are plenty of women who can give me what you're giving me here, sweetheart. You choose. Either you do exactly as I say, when I say it, sexually speaking, or this is over.'

He was bluffing, but for the first time since he'd met her he was doing it superbly. His face wasn't totally unreadable, but it remained convincingly hard and cruelly cold.

'Well? What's it to be?' he snapped.

She didn't say a word. She just glared at him, then turned her face away and stayed put.

Rico's moment of triumph felt somewhat shallow. Perhaps because underneath he knew only her pride was hurting. Underneath her outburst, she *wanted* to stay, not like a good little girl but like a bad little girl. A very bad little girl. This was the kind of fun and games she obviously liked. She just wasn't used to the man running the show. As he'd once thought, Renée liked being on top, not under a man's orders, or pushed up against a wall.

Rico determined not to hurry back despite it not taking more than thirty seconds to strip himself naked. He took his time going to the toilet, washing his hands, cleaning his teeth, applying some expensive cologne. He even contemplated having a shower but decided that might be going too far. After a good ten minutes his own frustration won the day so he slipped on his black silk bathrobe, sashed it then strode casually back down the carpeted hallway to the foyer.

She wasn't there. She'd gone. Fled. Escaped. Run out on him.

He swore, and was about to wrench open the front door and follow her—a rather stupid plan of action in his present attire—when he noticed that her things were still there. Her bags and her clothes. No way would she have taken the lift down to the lobby in the get-up he'd left her in. She'd be arrested for indecent exposure.

So where was she?

A door suddenly opened down the other hallway, the door to the guest bathroom, just this side of the study. Renée emerged then sashayed slowly back towards him, her eyes calm and composed.

He gulped at the sight of her in slow motion, his eyes riveted first at her still boldly bared breasts, then to the smooth naked mound between her thighs. All his controlling anger shattered, replaced by a desire so hot and so fierce that it frightened him.

'You were gone so long,' she explained coolly on reaching him. 'I simply had to go to the loo. I was desperate. Don't worry. I'll go right back to where I was, as ordered.'

When she went to brush past him his hand shot out to grab her nearest wrist, spinning her back then yanking her hard against him.

'Put your arms up around my neck,' he told her, which she did, eyes flaring wide, lips gasping apart.

With her wearing such high heels, there wasn't much between their height—Renée was a tall woman—so the juncture of her thighs was in just the right place for him. No time to waste now, he realised, the brakes he'd been exerting on his body up till now no longer working. He was beginning to lose control. His hands ripped open his robe, then moved down to push her legs apart, just wide enough for him to angle his erection away from his stomach and into the liquid heat between her legs. Dared he rub himself against her before slipping inside? He did, and the effect was well worth it. She stiffened against him, then cried out.

But not in pleasure. More in pain, the pain of knowing you were cripplingly close to coming. Did she feel like him? he wondered. Desperate to come but already resenting the moment of release.

'Look at me,' he whispered, and she did, just as he surged up into her.

'Oh,' she cried again, this time in stunned surprise.

He was big. Never bigger in fact. She'd done her job well, if this was what she wanted.

'Rico,' she sobbed.

'What?'

'Nothing. Just…just do it.'

Just do it. God, but he hated it when she said that. That was what she'd said last night. Didn't she know that this was special, him being inside her? That *she* was special, to *him*?

No, he thought savagely as he clamped his hands over her bare buttocks and began to pump up into her. She didn't know that. Any man would do, as long as he had the right equipment and knew how to use it. Use it and use *her*.

Her orgasmic cries were like daggers in his heart, as was the way her flesh convulsed violently around his. His immediate counter-climax was inevitable. How could he hold out against such stimulus?

But his own cries and shudders of physical ecstasy somehow shamed him. This was not how it should be between them. This was not what he wanted. He wanted to make love to her, not use her. Couldn't she understand that?

Obviously not. Her aim in all this—today at least—was sexual gratification. Which she was getting, if the length and intensity of her climax was anything to go by. Eventually, her body calmed and her arms sagged around his neck, her head drooping into the crook of his neck.

He reacted poorly when her mouth brushed his throat in a seemingly tender gesture. Hypocrite, he thought. She didn't want tenderness. She just wanted to be well and truly screwed.

When her knees started going out from under her,

he scooped her up and carried her down the hallway on the left, which led to the master bedroom. She wanted sex? She would get sex. She wanted to be in control for a change? He could do that, too. And he'd enjoy every single moment.

CHAPTER ELEVEN

RICO woke to the sound of the shower running, his head shooting up from the sheets to glance at the clock radio on the bedside table. Six fifty-three. He hadn't been asleep long. Only twenty minutes or so.

Relieved, he rolled over from where he'd been lying face-down on the bed, heaved himself up onto the pillows by the headboard, pulled a sheet up over his lower half, then hooked his arms behind his head.

Well, at least she hadn't run out on him this time. And why would she? He'd even surpassed his top-class performance of last night.

It had been five hours, give or take a few minutes, since they'd got here. Five hours and a lot of sex, and a lot of foreplay and afterplay in between. He'd used everything he'd ever learnt about women to keep her in a state of abandoned surrender.

Renée, he'd discovered to his surprise, *did* like to relinquish control. At least, with him she did. He'd been the one firmly in charge of the action, doing the seducing and the demanding and the taking. Yes, she'd been on top, but only at his command, and not for too long. He didn't want her getting ideas that she could be the boss in *his* bedroom. But she'd been a glorious sight, riding him, her head tipped back, her eyes shut, her mouth wide open as she gasped in much needed air. For a few moments he'd just lain back and watched her and wondered who she really was, this woman who captivated him so. Captivated and corrupted him.

Because this wasn't him, this dark and domineering master who was already planning more things to do to her, with only one ultimate aim in view: to coerce her into agreeing to be his permanent mistress, not just a passing one. If she wouldn't let him love her, then by God he was going to own her. He'd become a predator, a primitive, primal animal who'd found his mate and wasn't about to let her go. He had a month to stake his claim, to brand her, so to speak, to show her that he and only he could totally satisfy her. He would appeal to her dark side, and her intelligent side, but especially her female side, which seemed extra-vulnerable to his being a forceful lover. He must have tapped into some secret fantasy of hers, because a woman like Renée would not normally be so submissive, or co-operative. Yet not once had she said no to him this afternoon.

Oh, yes, soon he would have her exactly where he wanted her. Maybe not in love with him, but seriously in lust. Lust was almost as powerful as love, Rico believed. Sometimes even more powerful.

The water stopped running in the bathroom and his insides immediately tightened. Rico snorted in disgust at himself. So much for all his dark vows. He was the one who was afraid. Afraid of losing her.

What to do for the best? he worried. More sex at this juncture seemed like overkill. Better she be made to wait a while. Restoke her fires. And his fuel. He was just a man after all, not a machine.

He would take her out to dinner somewhere. That would kill two birds with one stone. Give them both a rest and force her to make small talk with him.

Talking could be just as effectively seductive—and as intimate—as lovemaking. Talking broke down defences, created bonds, dispensed with misconceptions and brought about understanding. Rico was dying to find out more about her. Maybe this was his chance, whilst she was all soft putty in his hands. Or she *had* been before he'd foolishly fallen asleep.

Yes, a good strategy that, taking her out to dinner.

He reached for the bedside phone and made a booking for seven-thirty at a nearby seafood restaurant where he was well known and wouldn't be turned down, regardless of his call coming so late on a Saturday afternoon. It was just a short walk away, down on the waterfront. He wouldn't have to drive, or worry over having a couple of glasses of wine.

By the time the bathroom doorknob turned ten minutes later, Rico was feeling reasonably confident about his plan of action for this evening. No sex for a while, just dinner and chit-chat. A good plan, till she actually walked back into the room, wrapped in one of his thick, thirsty navy bathsheets and looking like a bride the morning after her wedding night. Glowing was the word that sprang to mind. Glowing and gorgeous and, oh, goodness, there he went again.

She spotted the movement under the sheet straight away and shot him a shocked look. 'You can't be serious,' she said as she stared at the phenomenon. 'That's impossible!'

'Apparently not,' he said drily, hauling himself up into a sitting position against the headboard then lifting his knees to hide his erection. 'Just ignore it for now. I've booked us a table for dinner at seven-thirty. That gives you over an hour to be ready.'

'Ignore it,' she repeated, clearly agitated. She gave

a little shudder and lifted her eyes back to his face.
'What was that? Oh…oh, yes, dinner. I…I don't have
to get dressed up, do I? I've only brought casual
clothes with me and I don't want to wear that black
dress again. Or these,' she added, bending to scoop
up the corset, stockings and killer shoes from the
floor.

'Why not?' he asked.

'You know why not,' she snapped. 'Wearing them
did things to me. Bad things.'

'Wasn't that the idea when you bought them?' he
commented, thinking ruefully that she was back. The
old Renée.

'No.' She dumped everything on the chair next to
the bedside table, the one he sat on to put on his shoes
every morning. 'They were supposed to only do bad
things to *you*!'

He laughed.

'You can laugh. All that sexy stuff cost me a
bomb.'

'I did offer to recompense you but you refused.
Now, do stop complaining. You've been enjoying the
after-effects of your purchases all afternoon. So I'd
say they were a good investment, wouldn't you?'

Oddly enough, she aroused him more in what she
was wearing at this moment. Just one snatch of an
outstretched hand and she'd be standing there stark
naked. Rico had found earlier in the afternoon that he
preferred her that way. That corset had been a real
turn-on, no doubt about that. But nothing beat having
access to all of her body, every dip and curve, every
erogenous zone, every intimate, deliciously respon-
sive part. He loved stroking her smooth, soft stomach
and kissing it and, yes, rubbing his stubbly chin over

it. And elsewhere. She liked that, too. It had driven her wild.

Hell, stop thinking about sex, you fool, he ordered himself, painfully aware of the worsening situation in his nether region.

'You never did answer my question,' she said impatiently as she stood beside the bed and shook out her damp hair with her fingers, making it more tousled and incredibly sexy-looking.

'What question was that?' Rico replied coolly whilst his lower body raged white-hot. That short nap had certainly revived him.

'Can I wear trousers and a jumper to this place you've booked?'

'Sure. It's only casual. And it's only a five-minute walk from here. We won't have to leave till nearly half past seven.'

'Good. In that case, I'm going to go make some coffee before I get dressed. Would you like some?'

'Not right now. I'm heading for the shower myself.' A long cold one.

'Fair enough.' She turned and padded from the room in her bare feet, shaking her hair some more with her fingers as she went.

Rico bounced out of bed as soon as she was out of sight and headed, post-haste, for that hopefully life-saving shower. Five minutes later a teeth-chattering Rico switched off the icy water and grabbed the one remaining bathsheet, aware that the cold shower had worked all right. He'd not only lost his erection but everything else down there as well.

It seemed, however, that his neutering was only temporary, everything gradually dropping back to normal by the time he'd dried himself, sprayed on deodorant, combed his hair and cleaned his teeth.

'Now, I want you to behave yourself for a while,' he lectured his still twitchy penis as he slipped on the navy towelling robe he kept hanging on the back of the door. 'I'm trying to get to know the woman for the next few hours. And I'm not talking biblically here. So just cool it, will you?'

Rico was surprised when he re-entered the bedroom to encounter Renée there, standing over at the French doors, her hands clasped around a steaming mug of coffee, staring out at the view. An innocent enough sight. The trouble was that darned towel had slipped. Any more and her breasts would pop right out over the top, nipples and all.

'Down, boy,' he muttered under his breath.

'I'd go outside on the terrace,' she said on seeing him, 'and enjoy more of the views. But it's too cold. Nicely warm in here, though.'

And getting warmer by the minute, Rico thought irritably.

'I took myself on a brief tour around the other rooms after I made my coffee,' she went on. 'I hope you don't mind.'

'Not at all,' he said.

'I really like what you've done with the place. Your choice of furniture, I mean. I can see you haven't changed the wall colours or the carpet. But creams and greys go with just about anything, anyway, don't they? That red leather in the living areas looks fantastic, but I really love the rich, warm-coloured wood you've used in here,' she raved on, walking back to the bed, where she held her mug in one hand whilst she ran the other over the curved headboard. 'So much nicer than the bland cream-painted stuff Charles had.'

Rico blinked, then stared at her. It had never occurred to him till that second that Charles might have been one of Renée's past lovers. Yet, once it had, he could see that it was a distinct possibility. Till Charles had met and fallen in love with Dominique late last year, he'd been somewhat of a man about town. Frankly, he'd had more women than Rico, who was not the playboy Renée had always believed.

'Was Charles one of your lovers?' he asked, a huge lump forming in his throat at the thought of it. Please, anyone but Charles.

'What?' She glanced up from where she was caressing that stupid bloody headboard, her eyes momentarily off in some other world. Probably thinking about the last bed that had stood on this very spot, and the last man she'd screwed in it. His best friend!

Her dreamy expression cleared to one of exasperation. 'Oh, don't be silly. Of course not.'

'Then how come you know what this bedroom looked like when he lived here?'

'For pity's sake, Rico, I've been here several times over the past few years. To parties and to Charles' wedding more recently. I'm a woman, which means I'm a snoop. I peeked in here, all right?'

Sounded reasonable. Brother, was he relieved! 'I guess so. So why did you say of course he wasn't your lover. Is Charles too old for you, is that it? You like your lovers young, I suppose. Young and randy. They'd have to be to keep up with you.' As the jealous and insecure words tripped out of his mouth, Rico would have given anything to take them back. But too late. The damage had been done.

She took another sip of coffee, then sighed. 'Look, could we possibly not get into this kind of conversation? It's such a waste of time. I'm here with you now, and I'll be here whenever you want me to be here for the next month. I'm your mistress for that span of time. But that doesn't give you the right to give me the third degree about what lovers I've had in the past, or anything else. I'm happy to chat with you on a wide range of topics. Work. The weather. Religion. Politics. Your decor. And, of course, sex. But I will not discuss my personal life. Which includes my past.'

'I see,' he bit out, frustrated on all levels. Taking her to dinner clearly wasn't going to achieve what he'd hoped. Not if she stubbornly refused to open up to him on a personal level. They still had to eat, but no way was he going out with a hard-on like the one he was trying to hide. His masochism where Renée was concerned was now over. For the next month at least.

'OK,' he said, adopting a cavalier attitude. 'If that's the way you want it. In that case, put down that coffee, take off that towel and get your sweet fanny around here to me. Pronto!'

He enjoyed her shock, then took advantage of her hesitation, disposing of his own towel and showing her what was waiting for her. She stared. No doubt about it. Then swallowed convulsively. He could see the movements in her throat. When she licked her lips, he knew he had her.

'Do you do this to all your women?' she threw at him angrily.

'Do what?'

'Corrupt them.'

He had to laugh. 'No. Only green-eyed witches who've given me curry for bloody years. Now, put down that mug and do as you're told, mistress mine!'

She didn't move a muscle for a long moment. Then slowly, haughtily, she put down the mug and removed the towel, tossing it well away from her. It was the first time he'd seen her standing up in the nude. Heavens, but she was lovely. Tall and sleek, with long, elegant curves. A thoroughbred through and through. If she'd been a horse paraded around a sale-yard, she would have commanded top dollar.

What a pity he couldn't actually buy her.

Suddenly, he hoped that report would show she was in some financial difficulty. Then he might have some bargaining power to keep her in his bed. But somehow he doubted it. All he could count on with Renée was the next month, and this moment.

'Now come round here,' he commanded, his voice as thick as treacle.

She obeyed, walking as he imagined she'd once done on the catwalk, with long, slow strides and that snooty look on her strikingly sculptured face. She came right up to him, her lovely green eyes locked to his, flashing fire and defiance and, yes, hatred still.

'So what do you want me to do, lord and master? Should I just lie back, or do you want me on my knees, perhaps? I'm sure you'd like that. But lo and behold, he's suddenly not saying anything. Can't make up your mind, lover? Let me make it up for you.' And she dropped to her knees before him.

He watched, fascinated and appalled, as she stroked him with one hand whilst she cupped and squeezed him with the other. The pleasure was electric. Blinding. *Compelling!* When her head bent and her lips made intimate contact, he gasped, then groaned. How easy it would be to let her do this, take him all the way. He almost let her. He *did* let her for a while. Too long, almost. But at the last second, he grabbed her by the arms and hauled her to her feet. Was it decency? Or despair which stopped him? He wasn't sure. He just knew that he could not let her do that to him in anger. He only wanted that from her in the heat of her passion.

'No,' he growled when her stunned eyes questioned him. 'Not that. And certainly not like that. I...I want to make love to you, don't you understand?' he said, shaking her. 'I want to take you in my arms and kiss your breasts and whisper sweet nothings in your ear. I want...I want...'

He broke off his impassioned speech and just kissed her, kissed till, yes, she moaned and melted in his arms. They fell back onto the bed together, mouths still fused, limbs tangling, hands frantically seeking intimate places. There was no skilled foreplay on his part this time, just wild, urgent action. His mouth abandoned hers, only because he needed air. She seemed just as desperate, her legs lifting to wrap high around him, opening her body wide to his. He slipped inside her like a knife through hot butter, her muscles grabbing at him and pulling him in deep.

'Oh, God,' she groaned. 'Why am I letting you do this to me?'

'Do what?' he ground out through gritted teeth. 'What am I doing to you?'

'You're driving me insane,' she panted. 'This is crazy. I can't. Not again,' she moaned, but she grabbed at his buttocks, digging her nails in hard as she pulled him in even deeper, her rocking hips driving him on and on. 'Yes, yes,' she urged. 'Like that. I...Oh...' And she came with a rush.

He gasped, then tore her hands away and lifted them high, high above her head, stretching her upper body tight, then tighter. With a raw moan, he lowered his full weight onto her, his chest crushing her breasts flat between them, their straining stomachs glued to each other. Inside her, he forced himself to be still, wanting to wallow in her abandoned surrender. Why, he wasn't sure. Perhaps because this was the only moment when he felt superior to her.

But all the while she kept spasming fiercely around him, taking him inexorably closer to his own climax. It was a fight to the end, but she won, her name bursting from his lips as his body exploded, his heart bursting with emotion at the same time whilst his head whirled with dismay.

Driving *her* insane, was he? How ironic. Didn't she know that she'd driven him insane eons ago? Why else did making love to her never satisfy him? Why did he start thinking about the next time almost before this time was over? What name did you give such a self-destructive desire? Addiction? Obsession? *Love?*

He didn't know what to call it any more. All he knew was that Renée was going to be his woman. Not just for this weekend. Or this month. For a long, long time. He wanted her here, under his roof, in his bed, every night, and he would do everything in his power, use every trick in the book, by fair means or foul, to achieve that end.

CHAPTER TWELVE

'I'M NOT going to let you go, you know,' he told her as they sipped the very nice Chablis he'd ordered, and waited for their barramundi in lemon butter to arrive. They'd skipped the entrée and gone straight to the main course. Renée had claimed she never ate entrées. Rico just wanted to get her straight back home to bed, where at least he always felt on top of things. Once she'd put her clothes on—the classy but conservative ones she normally wore this time—she'd immediately changed back into the Renée he had difficulty handling.

'You're mine now, Renée,' he added with considerable bravado. 'All mine.'

Her wine glass had stilled, mid-air, for a moment, but then she laughed and took another sip. 'Watch it, Rico. Your Italian blood is showing.'

'Meaning what?' he snapped.

'Meaning Italian guys, I've noticed, have this tendency to be excessively jealous and possessive over the women they've—er—been with.'

He glowered over the table at her, feeling exactly what she accused him of feeling. Yes, he was jealous, *and* possessive. She'd given him her body so completely and with such intense passion that surely he could be excused for thinking she could never have been quite like that with any other man before.

Soon, she'd realise that he was as special to her as she was to him. Meanwhile, he simply *had* to find out more about her. He couldn't wait for that stupid report. Despite her proclaiming she would not talk about her personal life, she'd just given him an opening.

'You've had an Italian boyfriend before, have you?' he asked.

She sighed an exasperated-sounding sigh. 'Might I remind you, Rico, that you are *not* my boyfriend? See what I mean? Spend one night or two with an Italian and they think they own you. Now, could we change the subject, please?'

'*You* brought it up. Look, we have to talk about *something*. So you had an Italian boyfriend once. Big deal. Tell me about him.'

She sighed again, and started twisting her wine glass round and round in her hands. 'His name was Roberto,' she said at last. 'He was a model, like myself at the time. He was very handsome. Like you,' she added with a rueful flick of her eyes at him. 'And good in bed. Like you.' Another dry glance. 'And a total, *total* bastard.'

Rico waited for her to add, like you. But she didn't. Instead, her eyes shimmered momentarily before she lifted the wine glass to her lips and drained it dry.

'I think I need another drink,' she said, her voice cold and hard, her eyes alone betraying her distress.

Rico reached for the bottle, which was resting in a portable wine cooler by his elbow, all the while struggling not to show *his* emotions. But he wanted to kill this Roberto for being the one responsible for making his Renée like this, for making her hostile to him from the start, just because he was Italian.

'What did he do that was so bad?' he queried casually as he refilled her glass.

'It doesn't bear repeating in detail. Let's just say he was totally and utterly selfish.'

'I'm not *totally* and utterly selfish,' he pointed out with a covering smile. Instinct warned him to keep things very light or she'd clam right up.

'That's a matter of opinion.'

'I never leave you unsatisfied.'

'True. I'll give you that. But I'm not talking about sexual selfishness. I'm talking about the capacity not to know, or care, how other people feel.' She fixed him with an uncompromising gaze. 'One month, Rico. That's the deal. Don't, for a moment, think this is going to go on any longer than that.'

'What if you find *you* don't want it to end in a month's time?'

Her eyes glittered with dry amusement but its meaning eluded him. What did she find so funny? 'I don't have long relationships with *any* man any more, Rico. I certainly won't be having one with you.'

'Why? Because I'm Italian?'

'Because it's not what I want.'

Rico decided to play the only trump card he held in his hand at the moment. 'Then why did you ask me to marry you for your prize last night?'

She almost spilled her wine.

After her initial knee-jerk reaction she just sat there, frozen with shock, whilst he fished the sheet of notepaper out of his trouser pocket and handed it over to her. She put down her glass, a bit clumsily, then stared down at the clearly outlined words that she'd written with her own hand.

'Very clever,' she muttered, then crumpled the piece of paper into a small ball.

'Well?' he prompted impatiently when she declined to say any more. 'Care to explain that to me?'

'No,' she bit out. 'We had a deal, Rico, and you haven't honoured your part of it. You weren't supposed to know what I asked for.'

'Why not? What's the big secret? It's not as though you're madly in love with me. Which leaves what, Renée? Spite? Money? *Sex?* What motivated that request, I'd like to know?'

'It was just one-upmanship,' she snapped. 'I knew that you were going to ask me for sex, so I went one better. I regretted writing it the moment I had. It was a stupid thing to do. I was relieved when you won.'

Rico recalled that this was true. She *had* been relieved when he'd won, for whatever reason.

'So it wasn't my money you were after?'

Again, she looked taken aback. 'You know, Rico, that's the second time you've mentioned money. Look, I know you think I married Jo for his money and that you believe most good-looking women who marry rich men are gold-digging tramps, but trust me, I am not interested in your money. Aah, here comes our food…'

She was relieved again, Rico thought, this time by the arrival of their meals. She also hadn't denied that she'd married dear old Jo for *his* money.

Yet, strangely enough, Rico was beginning to believe that she hadn't. There was something innately honest about Renée. She was secretive, yes. But not devious. And there was a difference.

Rico fell to eating his meal whilst he decided on his next brilliant topic of conversation and had only taken a few mouthfuls of the mouth-watering barramundi when his cellphone rang.

'Should have turned the darned thing off,' he muttered as he fished the phone out of his pocket and answered.

'Rico,' was all his mother said, but it was enough for every nerve-ending in Rico's body to go on emergency alert.

'Yes, Mum, what is it?' he asked, trying not to sound sick with instant worry. But his voice must have betrayed a considerable amount because he'd never seen Renée look at him with such concern before.

'It's your *papa*,' his mother went on. 'He was having bad chest pains after dinner, but he didn't want me to do anything. He said it was just indigestion from my cooking. But he looked so bad, Rico. Bad colour. Bad breathing. I took no notice of Frederico for once and called the ambulance. I am at Liverpool Hospital now and the doctors, they…they are doing tests. They won't say much but they look worried, Rico. I think you should come. They will talk to you.'

'I'm on my way.'

He was already on his feet, his heart racing, panic a heartbeat away. Not his dad. Not yet. Not before he got there, at least.

'I have to go, Renée. My dad's in hospital with a suspected heart attack. I'm sorry. I just have to go.'

'I'm coming with you,' she said, and jumped up too.

'No. You won't be able to keep up. I have to run home and get my car first and I'm not going to slow down for anything.' He was already on his way, throwing a hurried explanation at the *maître d'* as he bolted past, breaking into a run as soon as he was outside.

You could have knocked him over with a feather when she not only caught up with him but also kept up with him, all the way to his apartment building. He didn't waste any energy asking her how till they were in the Ferrari and on their way. Even then, he didn't speak till they were forced to stop at a set of lights. He was too out of breath.

'Care to tell me how you managed that?' he asked her at this point. Hell, she wasn't even puffing!

'Running is my exercise of choice,' she replied. 'I go in the City-to-Surf fun run each year. And other fun runs. I'm one very fit gal.'

He nodded in wry agreement, not really wanting to talk. He'd just been curious.

'Just drive, Rico,' she said, surprising him with her insight. 'And don't speed. You don't want to have an accident, or get pulled over. That won't get you to your father's bedside any quicker, will it?'

His glance carried gratitude for her sense, and sensitivity. Then he just drove in concentrated silence, not speeding, but taking every short cut he knew, all the while trying to keep the panic at bay, reassuring himself with the thought that lots of heart-attack victims survived these days, if they got to the hospital in time. He just hoped his dad would be one of them. He prayed he would be.

The drive took forty minutes, with Rico not sure where to go when he got there. His stress level by this time was extreme, his decision-making powers not what they usually were.

'In there,' Renée advised, pointing to the casualty sign. 'That's where your father will be. You get out and I'll park the car for you. Then I'll come to Casualty and find you. OK?'

He did exactly that, stopping briefly to give her a peck through the window before he rushed off. 'Thanks,' he said.

'Good luck,' she called after him. 'I'll start praying for your dad.'

'You do that,' he called over his shoulder, then forged on into the casualty section. He'd already been praying all the way there.

It was bedlam inside, the waiting room chock-full of patients. Saturday night, of course, was the busiest night for any casualty section in a large hospital. It took some time for Rico to be seen to, then shown to where his father lay, eyes closed, ashen-faced, in a narrow hospital bed, his mother sitting by his side.

She looked very relieved to see Rico.

'How is he?' Rico asked straight away as he hugged her.

'I am fine,' his father answered grumpily, his eyes opening. 'I told your *mama* it was nothing. But she is a stubborn woman, and here I am, having lots of silly tests when I could be home, sitting in my favourite chair and watching my favourite television show.'

'What tests have they done?' he asked, directing the question at his mother. 'You be quiet and rest,' he ordered his father when he opened his mouth to answer. 'I'm talking to Mum here.'

'You are getting too big for your boots, Enrico,' his father muttered, but closed his eyes and fell silent.

'I don't know,' Teresa told her son worriedly. 'Lots of machines and wires and things. And they gave him some medicine. I don't know what.'

Rico swept up the chart from the bottom of the bed and did his best to decipher what was on it. Not easy.

Such a scrawl! 'Mmm. Looks like they did an ECG and an ultrasound. Blood pressure very high. I doubt it's just indigestion, Dad. But you don't seem to be dying just yet.'

'Mandretti men do not die before ninety,' his father retorted. 'Only if they are murdered.'

Teresa was startled by a soft laugh coming from a woman who had suddenly appeared beside her son at the foot of the bed. A tall, strikingly beautiful woman with jet-black hair and lovely green eyes and the nicest smile. Teresa was one of those people who either liked or disliked people on the spot. This woman, she liked.

But who *was* she?

'Aah, you found us,' Enrico said, turning to smile at the woman.

'I had to tell them I was your fiancée before they would let me in,' the woman returned, her pretty green eyes sparkling. 'I see your dad's not doing too badly. That's good. My prayers must have worked.'

Now Teresa liked her even more. A woman who prayed was not only nice, but also good.

'Mum, Dad, this is Renée. My horse-racing and poker-playing friend. We were having dinner together when you called, Mum. Renée was nice enough to come with me and stop me from getting a speeding ticket.'

Teresa could not have been more taken aback. *This* was Renée? Why, she didn't look a day over twenty-five! And she was nothing like her son's usual woman. Not blonde. Or bosomy. Or showy. And she'd been having dinner with her son. Must have come to her senses after all!

'It is lovely to meet you at last, Renée,' Teresa

replied, coming forward to give her a hug and a kiss on the cheek. 'I have heard so much about you from Enrico, but you look so much younger than I pictured. You must come and visit us at home soon. Isn't that right, Papa?'

'*Sì*. If I ever get out of here.'

'Well, that won't be tonight, Mr Mandretti,' the doctor said as he bustled in. 'We will be wanting to keep a close eye on you for a couple of days yet. Now…'

Whatever he was going to say was interrupted by the noisy arrival of Katrina, Teresa's youngest daughter and the apple of her father's eye. Katrina was the only other one of her offspring whom Teresa had rung, not wanting Frederico to be overwhelmed by visitors and noise. But Teresa knew that Katrina would never have forgiven her if she hadn't been notified at once that her beloved *papa* was ill. Unfortunately, Katrina had brought her youngest child with her, Gina, who was four and given to crying at the drop of a hat.

Gina took one look at her grandpapa in bed and started howling.

'Hush, darling. Hush,' Katrina said, looking very harassed. 'Sorry, Mama, but Paulo had to work tonight and I couldn't leave Gina with the other kids. They don't know how to handle her.'

Rico was of the opinion that no one could handle Gina. Katrina certainly couldn't. Spoilt through and through, that child was.

'Here. Let me take her,' Renée offered, and scooped the wailing child out of his sister's highly ineffectual hands. 'I'm Renée,' she told an open-mouthed Katrina.

'My fiancée,' Rico added drily, then laughed when Katrina's mouth fell even more open. 'I'll explain later.'

'And I'll be out in the waiting room,' Renée said.

Katrina's head swivelled from one to the other. 'But…but…'

'Don't worry,' Renée reassured her. 'I'm very good with children.'

Rico could see it was a statement of some truth, since the little devil had immediately stopped crying. Renée was constantly amazing him tonight.

'Thanks again,' he said.

She smiled, then walked off, chatting away to the child in her arms as she went. Rico stared after her for a second before dragging his mind back to his father's health. That had to be his first priority at this moment, even though it did look as if his dad wasn't in any immediate danger.

The doctor told the family that Rico's father had had *not* a heart attack but a serious angina attack, the forerunner of a coronary. The plan was to move him shortly to a cardiac ward, where he would be kept for observation and treatment for a couple of days, during which time he would be seen by a specialist as well as a cardiac-care consultant. A change in lifestyle and diet would undoubtedly be prescribed, which brought a scowl from Rico's father and a quick rebuke from his mother.

'You will do what the doctors say,' she said firmly. 'You are the one who is stubborn. Not me.'

'And I'm going to buy you a couple of grey-hounds,' Rico butted in. 'Then you can walk them. Get your heart as fit as a fiddle and have some fun at the same time.'

'Walking and fun is excellent therapy for the heart,' the doctor concurred. 'You should listen to your wife and son, Mr Mandretti. They know what's best for you.'

Rico's father pulled a face. '*Sì, sì.* Enrico always thinks he knows best. If he is so clever then why didn't he marry that lovely lady who was just here, instead of that other one with the bleached hair and that silly laugh?'

Rico winced at this reminder that Jasmine had had a silly laugh. A high-pitched giggle that had been as false as the rest of her.

'I'll be back,' the doctor said, then scuttled off. No rest for the wicked, Rico thought, or Casualty doctors.

'But he *is* going to marry her, isn't he, Papa?' Katrina piped up, sounding puzzled. 'He said she was his fiancée.'

'Was just a silly joke,' the old man said scornfully. 'She does not want to marry this clever boy. Your *mama* told me so.'

Rico glowered at his mother, then scowled at himself. Because she was right. Renée didn't want to marry him.

Or *did* she?

She had asked him to marry her in that bet, hadn't she? OK, so she claimed it was one-upmanship, and that did ring true, given their history. But what if something else had been at play there? What if…?

For the first time, Rico began to consider the possibility that something was going on with Renée that he'd been blind to. Ali might have touched upon it when he said that what some women say and what they *feel* were two different things.

Rico had hard evidence of what Renée *felt* for him

when she was with him in bed, when her defences were down. Not just desire and need, but also passion. A deep and powerful passion, which drove her body to feel things that her mind resisted.

'I shouldn't be letting you do this to me…'

That was what she'd said shortly after she'd acted as if she didn't want to make love with him; that she was only obeying because she'd lost the bet.

But her body had been on fire for him. Her body had been on fire for him all along. Why? What would make a woman like Renée want a man so much if she supposedly hated him?

And then the solution came to him. The other side of hate. Love.

She's in love with me!

The thought blew his mind.

Could it possibly be true?

She would deny it, of course, even if it *was* true. Maybe she didn't even recognise what she really felt, as he hadn't recognised the truth of his feelings for her up till tonight. Maybe her silly pride was getting in the way, or those old tapes she had in her head about Italian men.

Rico frowned and fretted over this last very real problem. He had to make her see that not all Italian men were like Roberto. He had to make her see that it wasn't just sex he wanted from her, but a future as well. A future and a family. She wasn't too old to have children. Not at all. She…

'Enrico,' his mother said, laying a gentle hand on his arm, 'The people are here to wheel your father's bed away.'

'Oh. Oh, sorry, Mum. I was off in another world.'

'I know…' She smiled one of her soft, understanding smiles. 'Perhaps you should go check how your Renée is doing with Gina.'

Their eyes met, mother and son.

She knows, Rico realised. Knows how I feel about Renée.

She patted his arm and smiled. 'Go to her and wait with her till your *papa* is settled in his room. And then the three of you can come, visit with him for a while. *Sì?*'

'*Sì,*' Rico agreed, and bent to kiss her cheek. 'Love you. Be with you soon, Dad,' he added more loudly. 'Don't worry about, Gina,' he told his sister. 'She'll be fine.'

Teresa watched her son hurry off, and for a moment her heart was full of sorrow. I've really lost him this time, she was thinking. He belongs to her now.

'Teresa,' came the oddly fragile plea from the bed, and she turned to see her husband of almost fifty years looking at her as he had never looked at her before. With fear in his eyes.

She hurried over and took his hand in hers. It felt cold, and old. 'It's all right, Frederico. I'm here. And you are going to get well. I will see to it myself.'

His face registered surprise, then pleasure. '*Sì*, Teresa. I know you will. A good woman, your *mama*,' he said to his daughter. 'A very good woman…'

Not so good, Teresa was thinking. A silly, selfish old *mama* who has finally grown up.

CHAPTER THIRTEEN

Rico found Renée in a far corner of the waiting room, talking to a thankfully quiet Gina, who was sitting on the plastic chair next to her and staring with rapt attention up into Renée's face. As Rico drew closer he could hear she was telling the child a story.

'And the big bad wolf put on one of Grandma's nighties and jumped into Grandma's bed just as Little Red Riding Hood…'

Renée broke off once she saw Rico, with the child immediately protesting. Rico swept a wailing Gina up from her chair and sat down with the child placed firmly in his lap.

'If you don't shut up, Gina,' he warned with deep authority in his voice, 'you won't hear the rest of the story.'

It was the right thing to say. Gina shut up immediately.

'Do go on,' he encouraged Renée. 'This is one of my favourites.'

'I imagine you like all stories that star big bad wolves,' she quipped drily before continuing.

Rico laughed, then listened. What a natural storyteller she was! He was impressed.

Unfortunately so was Gina, who wanted another one as soon as *Little Red Riding Hood* was finished. Renée launched into *The Three Little Pigs* without batting an eyelid, clearly knowing that story equally well. Fortunately, this time, Gina began to droop during the telling, and was sound asleep shortly after the last *I'll huff and I'll puff and I'll blow your house down*.

Renée immediately stopped and *Rico* protested. 'I've come this far. I want to hear the end.'

She gave him a droll look. 'You mean the bit where the big bad wolf gets his comeuppance?'

'Absolutely.'

'Mmm. What a pity real life doesn't echo fairy stories. I know a big bad wolf who could do with falling into a pot of boiling water. Scald his ego a bit.'

'Ouch. But seriously, though, Renée, how come you know these stories so well? You didn't miss a beat.'

'That's because I spent a good chunk of my teen-age years reading those stories to my much younger cousins every single night.'

'How come?'

'How come? I was brought up by my aunt and uncle from the age of twelve.'

'How come?'

She sighed. 'You ask a lot of questions.'

'I'm interested.'

'I know *exactly* what you're interested in where I'm concerned, Rico Mandretti. But I suppose you can't indulge that appetite here so you want to feed your curiosity instead. Very well, if you must know. When I was twelve, I became an orphan. My parents were killed in a head-on collision, along with my younger sister. I was luckily—or unluckily, depending on your point of view—staying with my aunt and uncle that day. They took me in afterwards and I lived with them till I left school and came to Sydney to find work.'

'You weren't happy with them, though, were you?' Rico said, reading between the lines.

Renée shrugged. 'They did their best for me, I suppose. I mean…I wasn't their daughter, just a niece. But my aunt was not a motherly woman. Lord knows why she had baby after baby. I do know she liked having a ready-made baby-sitter in me. I looked after those babies from sun-up to sun-down some days. Not that I minded all that much. Her kids loved me, even if she didn't. And I needed someone to love me back then.'

Rico was shocked, both by her tragic story and the fact that till that moment he hadn't given a serious thought to Renée's family or her upbringing. Yet he claimed he loved her. Maybe he *was* as selfish as her other Italian lover. Or maybe *all* men were selfish. Whatever, it was high time he started thinking about her, instead of himself.

'You haven't mentioned your uncle. You didn't have any trouble with him, I hope.'

She looked startled. 'What do you mean? Oh…oh, no, not at all. Why do people always think awful things like that?'

Rico shrugged. 'It's just that you must have been a very good-looking girl, even at twelve.'

'Actually no, I wasn't. I never was the cute and pretty type, with baby-blue eyes and curls et cetera. I was always very thin and bony, with straight, mousy-brown hair, skin that didn't tan and these big pale green eyes. My nickname at school was Froggie. Then, around fourteen, I shot up far too quickly and became terribly awkward and gangly. All legs and no bust to speak of. I wasn't the kind of young girl that men look at and lust over. By the time I was eighteen

I'd improved somewhat, but I still had no style or poise. I used to go round with my shoulders hunched and looking down at the ground all the time.'

'I find that hard to believe. You walk so beautifully now. So proudly.'

'Thanks to a deportment and grooming course I was lucky enough to win after I came to Sydney. It was a prize in a raffle the women were running at work for charity. I was the mail girl at a plastics factory at the time. Anyway, the people running the course said I had the right look for a model and recommended me to an agency. I never expected to be taken on but I was, and in no time I was on the catwalk and doing fashion layouts. I never reached supermodel status—I'm not quite tall enough for that— but I did very well for myself.'

'I have to confess I only vaguely recall your name. But then, I wasn't into dating models.'

'Not enough boob for your taste?'

'Very funny. No. I think my ego was too large to compete with successful women. I was content with girls who said I was wonderful all the time, not the other way around. Hopefully, I've grown up a bit since then. I know you think I go from one blonde bimbo to another but that's not true. Not any more, anyway.'

She threw him a thoughtful look. 'You surprise me, Rico. It's a sign of real maturity to be able to look back at things you've done and understand why you've done them. I'm really glad you're not going to go back to dating girls like Jasmine. You deserve better.' Is this *me* saying *that*? Well, I did say you were driving me insane.'

Their eyes met and he wanted to kiss her again.

Very badly. But, of course, he didn't. Instead, he decided to press on with finding out more about her.

'So how did your parents' accident happen?' he asked gently. 'Under what circumstances?'

Her eyes saddened with the memory. 'Mum and Dad had to take my little sister, her name was Fay, to Sydney to see a specialist. She had scoliosis of the spine. We lived out in the country, on a farm, not far from Mudgee. Not many specialists out there. They'd driven down to Sydney early that morning, and been at the hospital all day. They stayed for a meal and didn't start the drive back till it was quite late. They weren't all that far from home when their car veered onto the wrong side of the road straight in front of a truck. They think Dad fell asleep at the wheel.'

Rico's heart went out to her. 'That's tough, Renée. Really tough. I'm so sorry.'

Their eyes connected and he hoped she would see genuine sympathy in his.

'You're not really a big bad wolf, are you?' she said with a frown.

He smiled, happy that she could see beyond the playboy tag at last. 'No. But I haven't been at my best the last couple of days. I have to admit that.'

'Wow, if that's not your best then I'm in for a few treats during the next month.'

Rico had to laugh. She had a wicked sense of humour. He was almost tempted to tell her right then and there that she didn't fool him. He *knew* she wanted more from him than sex. She wanted him to love her. *And* to marry her.

But it was neither the right time nor the right place for such a confrontation. He didn't want to risk losing her altogether by being impatient. He would wait till the time *was* right, till she was ready to accept his love. Meanwhile, he would keep on carefully asking her about herself. She'd started to tell him things now. There was no reason for her to stop.

'So what are they doing with your dad?' she asked first. 'He didn't look too bad from what I saw. A bit pasty-faced but well able to live till that ninety he said you Mandretti men live to. Unless they're murdered, of course. By jealous exes and vengeful mistresses, no doubt.'

He grinned, and was proceeding to update her on what the doctor had said when Katrina made an appearance, looking both surprised and pleased when she saw her little girl was asleep.

'I was getting worried,' she said. 'I see I didn't have to be. Thank you so much, but I'd better take Gina home now,' she went on, easing the child out of Rico's arms into her own. 'Papa's resting comfortably. I'll come and see him tomorrow. Nice to meet you, Renée. And thanks for minding Gina. I'm sorry you're not Rico's real fiancée. He could do with marrying someone nice for a change. Bye, Rico.' She bent to kiss him, whispering, 'You silly fool,' as she did so.

He grinned up at her as she straightened. Katrina had been like a second mother to him as he grew up and had spoiled and indulged him almost as much as she had Gina. For her to call him a silly fool was a very serious rebuke indeed. But it meant she approved of Renée as a potential sister-in-law.

He liked that idea. A lot.

'See you tomorrow, sis.'

She rolled her eyes at him and left.

'Are all your brothers and sisters as good-looking as you are?' Renée asked as Katrina walked off.

Rico thought about that for a second. 'Almost,' he said, and Renée punched him playfully on the upper arm. 'You're an arrogant sod.'

'Yeah. It's a problem we big bad wolves have in common. We're arrogant. So, shall we go see what the old man is up to?' He stood up and took her hand, pulling her to her feet.

'Would you prefer for me to wait for you in the car?'

'Absolutely not. Dad's always had an eye for a pretty woman. Seeing you again will keep his ticker going.'

'Flatterer.'

'That's another quality you can rely upon in a big bad wolf. We're all flatterers.'

'I already said you *weren't* a big bad wolf.'

'So you did. In that case, I'm not a flatterer. You must be really pretty, then.'

She gave him one of her droll looks. 'Lead on, Mr Mandretti.'

'I'll have to ask the nurse at the desk for directions first.'

He asked the nurse, got directions, then set off for the ward they'd moved his father to. The directions were rather complicated, and they got lost a couple of times, wandering down empty and echoing corridors before finally reaching the wing, and the right room. Rico was pleased to see it was a private room with only one bed in it. His father looked very settled, and much better, with some colour in his face. He was also sound asleep, courtesy of an injection he'd been given, his mother told them.

'There's no need for you to stay,' she told Rico. 'Come and visit tomorrow.'

'But what about you, Mum? You should get some sleep. I'll drive you home.'

'Thank you, Enrico, but no. They say I can stay. A nice nurse is going to bring in a stretcher bed. I sleep in here by your *papa*.'

Rico frowned. He didn't like the sound of that. It worried him. Why would the hospital let his mother do that? Unless it meant...

'It's fairly standard procedure these days in hospitals,' Renée broke in softly. 'Don't worry.'

He looked at her. 'How did...?' He shook his head. 'Never mind.' He liked to think she was sensitive to his needs, that they were already becoming attuned to each other, not just physically but emotionally. He gave his mother a goodbye hug and his father a kiss goodbye, just in case.

'Don't die on me, Dad,' he whispered. 'I love you.'

'He'll be all right,' Renée said as they walked together back to his car, Renée leading the way. 'He's in good hands.'

'I guess so.'

'But you'll worry all the same,' she said as they reached the Ferrari, which was standing alone in the main car park under a lit telegraph pole. 'You love your family a lot, don't you?'

'But of course. Family is everything, Renée.'

Her eyes turned instantly bleak and he could have kicked himself. 'Oh, God, I *am* a fool,' he muttered, and pulled her into his arms.

She went willingly, but with a sob. When she buried her face against his chest and wept, he just held her and stroked her hair. 'I shouldn't have said that,' he said regretfully. 'It was stupid of me.'

'No,' she choked out, shaking her head. 'No, it was beautiful.' And then she wept some more. Deeply. Despairingly.

He let her cry herself out, knowing that there was nothing he could say to make her feel better. Before tonight, he would have had no concept of what it felt like to lose both your parents so tragically. Going through this scare with his father had given him some idea. But not entirely, he conceded. How could he possibly know how she'd felt as a twelve-year-old, being told that her whole family had been snuffed out? And then having to live with people who didn't really want or love you?

'I don't know about you,' he said when she finally stopped crying. 'But I could do with something to eat. Do you think they might have kept our barramundi warm?'

'Why don't we go to my place instead?' she offered, her eyes still looking lovely despite their red rims. 'I have a whole heap of ready-made meals in my freezer that wouldn't take long to heat up in the microwave. Not supermarket muck, either. Good food that I've cooked myself.'

'Sounds great to me,' he said, hiding his surprise that she bothered to cook at all.

Her town-house was even more of a surprise. Country-style furniture and very comfy, where he'd envisaged either ultra-expensive antiques or that cold, minimalist stuff you saw in style magazines. In no time he was sitting on floral-cushioned wooden chairs and forking spicy Thai chicken and noodles into his eager mouth, washed down with some refreshing Chinese tea.

'You've no idea how much I enjoy eating food other people have cooked,' he said between mouthfuls.

'You've no idea how much I enjoy seeing someone else *eat* my cooking,' she countered. 'It's always just me.'

He let that information sink in whilst he downed some more of the simply delicious food. There was so much he didn't know about her.

'Why did you marry a man so much older than yourself, Renée?' he asked when both their plates were empty. 'And please…don't give me some bull-dust answer. I want the truth.'

'The truth,' she repeated slowly, then leant back in her chair, her face taking on a resigned expression. 'You really are extra-curious tonight, aren't you? All right. Perhaps it's time you heard the truth, anyway. I married Jo because he loved me. And because he didn't want children.'

Rico could not have been more startled. Or more worried.

'It had absolutely nothing to do with his money,' she added wryly.

'Fine.' Rico nodded slowly. 'OK. I believe you. But why didn't *you* want children?'

'I didn't say that, Rico. I said *Jo* didn't.'

'I'm sorry. I'm confused.' Utterly.

'I am only telling you this because I have an awful feeling where all this is heading. The total truth is, Rico, I *can't* have children.'

Her baldly delivered statement struck him like a physical blow, obliterating in one fell swoop everything he had been planning. How could he marry her and make her the mother of his children if she couldn't have any?

Rico sat there with his mouth hanging open and his hope for their future together disintegrating on the spot.

'How...how long have you known?' he asked at last, when he could think again.

'Since I was twenty-six. I had an ectopic pregnancy. Twins. One in each tube. There were complications, along with a severe bacterial infection. After the operation necessary to save my life, I was told the good news.'

Rico didn't know what to say. He knew her sarcasm hid a lot of pain. He could see it in her eyes. The surgeon must have had to give her a hysterectomy. Dear God, what devastating news for a woman in her twenties!

But it explained so much. Her marriage to Joseph Selinsky. Her decision to never have a real relationship since becoming a widow. Her reluctance to talk, or even *think* of love.

'Roberto was the father, wasn't he?' he said with further insight.

'How did you guess?'

'So what happened? He just dumped you after he found out you couldn't have any more children, was that it?'

'Heavens, no, Roberto was much more selfish than that. He pretended to be sympathetic. Told me it didn't matter, that he still loved me madly and we would still get married. He continued to sleep with me. Naturally. But he began going overseas a lot. Modelling assignments, he told me. Around that time,

I started up the modelling agency and soon found out through contacts that Roberto hadn't been working in the business for ages. He was away when I discovered this piece of puzzling news. I rang him immediately and tackled him over what was going on. He confessed over the phone that he'd been spending all his time in Italy with his new wife, his new *pregnant* wife.'

Rico sucked in sharply. The bastard went and got himself married!

'She was from a very wealthy family,' Renée continued, then smiled a travesty of a smile. 'The funny thing is he could not understand why I was so upset. He said I couldn't possibly expect him to really marry me. He said he still loved me and wanted me to continue being his lover. He said his father-in-law was in the shoe business and had given him a job in the export-sales division and that he would be coming to Australia regularly on business. He said it was a perfect arrangement and I was perfect mistress material, since I could not conceive and he wouldn't even have to bother with condoms. He promised me he would only sleep with me and his wife so everything would be perfectly safe.'

Rico could hardly believe what he was hearing. What kind of man did something like that? Or said such amazingly arrogant and incredibly insensitive things?

'So…what did you do?'

'What do you mean, what did I do?' she flung back at him. 'I told him to go screw himself and that if he ever came near me again I'd cut his balls off with a carving knife! What do you think I did?' she said, jumping up, her voice having risen hysterically. 'Do you think I just lay back and let him do what he liked when he liked? Give me credit for more pride than that. The only reason I'm telling you this is so that you won't go getting any silly ideas about my marrying you. Which you have been thinking of tonight, haven't you? You think you love me. You probably think I love you. And maybe I do. But whether I do or not is totally irrelevant, under the circumstances. You want children. I can't give them to you. End of story. End of affair.'

He stood up, walked round and took her trembling body into his arms. 'I don't just *think* I love you, Renée. I *know* I love you. I've always loved you. I love you and I want you to be my wife. To hell with your not being able to have children. They're secondary to what I feel for you.' And he meant it. How could he possibly do what Roberto had done? Marry some other woman, just to have children, when all the while his heart belonged to *this* woman, this incredibly brave, beautiful, proud, stubborn woman?

'No, they're not,' she wept. 'They're not secondary. They're one of the most important things to you. And you *don't* love me. Not really. It's just sex. Give you a solid month of sleeping with me, night after night, and this so-called love you feel will burn a little less brightly and you'll be grateful that I didn't say I'd marry you tonight. Even if you did really love me, any marriage between us is still doomed. You'd end up hating me.'

'I doubt that. I've already tried hating you and it didn't work. It didn't work for you, either. We love each other, Renée, and nothing is ever going to change that. We love each other and we should be together as man and wife. As for children...we can adopt them. I know there aren't many children up for adoption in Australia but there are other parts of the world where poor, neglected orphan kids are crying out for a good mum and dad. And we'll make very good parents.'

She stared up into his face, her green eyes luminescent with tears, and something else. It was wonder. Wonder and awe.

'You really mean that, don't you?'

'I do.'

'Oh, God, how…how can I say no? Yet I should say no. I know I should. This is all too quick. Too soon. You…you aren't thinking quite straight at the moment. Look, I'll make you a new deal. I'll be your mistress for the next month, as agreed. A month of wild, uncontained and constant sex, Rico. And then, after that month is up, if you still want me to marry you, I will.'

'No kidding?' Rico had difficulty containing his elation over her agreement, not about her promise of all that wild, uncontained and constant sex. Although, damn it all, that sounded pretty good too.

'No kidding.'

'You won't go back on that?' he growled, sweeping her up off the floor into his arms.

'Not unless you do something really terrible in the meantime.'

'Like what?'

'I don't know. Turn into a serial killer or start shaving on the weekends, perhaps,' she murmured, reaching to run her hand over his very stubbly cheek and chin. 'I think my nipples have become addicted to this…'

'Only your nipples?' he said wryly.

'Perhaps some other sensitive little bits as well.'

'You know nothing about addiction, lady,' Rico growled and started to carry her towards her bedroom. 'Let me show you what serious addiction is, and the only way to deal with it.'

Rico was making love to her for a second time when he suddenly remembered those reports he had commissioned.

'Rico,' she moaned softly when he stopped moving.

He kissed her shoulder. 'Just taking a breather, darling.'

God help him, he thought, if she ever found out. Should he ring Keith up tomorrow and cancel them? Not much point, really. What difference would that make now? Besides, he still wanted to know who she'd been sleeping with. And no way would Renée tell him that. As far as her finances were concerned…maybe he should put his mind totally at rest there as well.

'Rico…please…' Her hips wriggled against his, her breasts jiggling under his hands.

He groaned. Impossible to think of other things right at this moment.

His right hand slid down to splay over her stomach, his left staying clamped to her left breast. He pressed her back against him till they were two perfect spoons, curved around each other, their flesh as one. When she wriggled again, sharp flashes of electric pleasure shot through him. He was close to coming again. He rolled over onto his back and took her with him, his penetration not as deep now. When her legs moved restlessly apart and she continued her wriggling, he stayed very still inside her. Only his hands moved, his left playing with her fiercely erect nipples, his right moving down to where he knew she would be equally swollen.

Just the slightest touch there, and she gasped. A firmer stroke and she froze. A squeeze, and she cried out, then splintered apart.

'Mine,' he muttered, then came just as violently.

Mine…till death us do part.

Or until…

No, no, Rico vowed despairingly. That could not happen. He would not *let* that happen. Not now. Not ever! It would be his secret, carried with him to the grave.

CHAPTER FOURTEEN

RICO left the two reports on his glass-topped coffee-table and walked over to the corner bar to pour himself a drink. Selecting a heavy-based glass from the built-in shelves under the black granite bar-top, he half filled it with Glenfiddich, then added a few cubes of ice from the tray in the bar bridge. His hands shook as he did so.

Nerves.

Glass in hand, he made his way out onto the terrace, where he leant on the railing, sipped the whisky and tried to pull himself together. Dusk was falling and the city lights were rapidly blinking on. The evening promised to be coolish, with the night sky clear and dark and star-filled.

The quay below was still very busy with ferries leaving at regular intervals, carrying city workers home across the harbour. It was Friday, so lots more people had probably stayed on in town for end-of-week drinks and general carousing.

Renée was due home soon from a business trip to Melbourne. Unavoidable, she'd told him late last Monday as she'd headed for the airport. A staff emergency in the Victorian branch. He'd wanted to go with her but she'd said no, definitely not. Business and pleasure did not mix. Besides, she'd be back in a day or two. Each morning this week she'd promised to return that night, and each time something else had delayed her. But there would be no delay tonight, she'd assured him from Tullamarine Airport. She was on the six-o'clock flight and would catch a taxi straight from Mascot.

He'd missed her terribly these last four days. Renée had been virtually living with him since the beginning of their month's agreement three weeks back, only returning to her place to feed her goldfish and replenish her wardrobe. Her absence this week had highlighted to him how much he'd already come to depend on her company every night. And he didn't mean just the sex, although that continued to be incredible.

Rico understood, however, that their mutual urges to make love several times a night—or at regular intervals during the day at weekends—would eventually fade. They would not spend the rest of their lives unable to keep their hands off each other. Their love life would settle down to a more normal routine. Eventually.

That was why he was thrilled with how well they got along during their other times together. Charles and Dominique were astounded when they went to dinner at their place recently and didn't throw a single verbal dagger at each other, although Renée still liked to stir him a bit during their poker-playing evenings. They even behaved themselves at the races, not a difficult task so far, considering Ebony Fire had won brilliantly the last two Saturdays. Renée's pride and pleasure in her beloved Blackie had been touching to see. She'd cried with happiness. Rico understood that her horses were like the children she would never have, a situation he aimed to remedy. He'd already instructed his solicitor to investigate countries where legal adoptions could be fast-tracked.

Yes, all Rico's plans were falling into place. He had no doubt that Renée loved him, although she never said she did. And he had no doubt she would say yes to his proposal at the end of the month.

That was why, Rico realised as he downed his whisky in agitated gulps, he was so nervous at this moment. The woman he loved more than life itself would walk in the front door shortly. And what was he going to do? Risk his future with her by showing her those two reports, by confessing what he'd done.

He'd tossed and turned over this decision for the last few nights and found he could no longer live with the secret. Or his own curiosity. Frankly, the reports from the detective agency had created as many questions as they had solved. Not that they revealed anything bad. Just the opposite. The woman had to be a damned saint.

Yet Renée wasn't a saint. Who was?

The sound of the glass door sliding back behind him had Rico whirling round, the ice clinking in his glass.

'I didn't hear you come in,' he said, aware that he sounded strained.

Renée stayed standing in the doorway. 'I can see that. What's that you're drinking. Bourbon?'

'No, whisky. Would you like one?'

'Mmm. That would be nice. Flying always makes me strung-up.'

He felt her puzzled eyes on him as he brushed past and hurried over to the bar, where he mixed her a drink the way she liked it before dinner in the evenings. Whisky and ice, with a little soda.

'So what's made *you* so strung up?' she asked

when he handed her the drink. 'Something go wrong with your shooting schedule this week?'

'No. It went off like clockwork. Come and sit down, Renée. I have something I want to tell you and I don't think it can wait.' He knew if he procrastinated at all, he might wimp out. And that just would not do.

'Mmm. Sounds serious. Let me just get out of this jacket first,' she said, putting her drink down on the coffee-table right next to the reports and taking off the very tailored navy pinstriped jacket that went with the equally tailored trousers she had on. Underneath was a three-quarter-sleeve white shirt, which still looked crisp and smart, despite her travelling. Her hair was pulled back into a tight roll, and she was wearing a single string of pearls around her throat, along with simple matching earrings.

She looked chic and sexy, and Rico wanted desperately to change his mind and not do this and make love to her instead. But that would be the coward's way out.

'What's all this?' she asked, nodding towards the two reports as she picked up her drink again.

'It's what I wanted to tell you about,' he said.

'Oh?' Before he could stop her she'd put down her drink again, picked up the top report and started reading.

'Renée, please don't be angry,' he jumped in just as her head whipped up and around, her eyes blinking wide.

'You had me investigated,' she said disbelievingly. 'Like you had poor Dominique investigated.'

'Not quite.' With Dominique he'd asked them to

go right back, to the day the woman was born. 'There were just a few things I needed to know.'

'I can't believe this,' she raged, shaking the report at him. 'Why, you…you…'

'*Listen* to me before you go off at half-cock,' he ground out, hoping to sound firm and not panic-stricken. 'This was something I put into motion the morning after our first night together, immediately after I found out you'd asked me to marry you. That threw me, Renée. I couldn't work out why you'd ask for marriage. I was worried that your motive might have been money. I didn't know the real you then. Hell, I knew next to *nothing* about you. I still believed you'd married your last husband for money.'

'So what do you believe now?' she asked him with cold fury in her eyes. 'Are you satisfied after seeing this that I have enough money of my own? Or do you think I'm still looking for another gravy train to jump onto?'

'I'm satisfied you are a very wealthy but wonderful woman who gives heaps of money to charities and chooses to live reasonably simply. Other than the racehorses, of course. They cost a pretty penny. Try to understand, Renée, this was more about my emotional baggage than you. After Jasmine, I'd lost faith in beautiful women. When I met Charles' wife-to-be, *and* you, all I saw were two more mercenary gold-diggers willing to trade their bodies for financial security. You have to be honest, Renée. Both you *and* Dominique had bad track records. You can't blame me entirely for thinking what I did in the first place.'

She grimaced, then sighed, most of the anger leaving her face, replaced by reluctant agreement. 'No, I guess not. But you could have *asked* me, Rico, not set some professional to snoop into my finances and…and…' She broke off suddenly, then spun round to snatch up the next report, starting to read it before Rico had a hope of stopping her. He waited with trepidation for the next explosion.

It wasn't long in coming. Her head shot up, her face flushed. 'My God, you even had my personal life investigated! My…my *sex* life!'

'Only for the last five years,' he said apologetically.

'There is no *only* about this, Rico. This is unforgivable!' she said, throwing both reports onto the coffee-table and sweeping her drink back up with shaking hands. 'You must know that. Quite unforgivable. And downright typical.' She took a swift swallow of the whisky and soda. 'Bloody Italian men. You just can't trust them. Not a one. They don't love or trust you. They just want to own you and know all your sexual secrets and…and…'

'But you don't *have* any sexual secrets, Renée,' he pointed out, trying to stay calm in the face of her fury. 'You haven't *had* a sex life. Not since your husband died. There have been no men in your life during that time. Why, Renée? I want to know.'

'Oh, do you, now? Well, bully for you! I would have thought, being typically Italian, that you'd be pleased as punch that I'd been celibate all this time. I could almost qualify as a born-again virgin. You Italians like virgins, so I've gathered. Roberto wasn't at all pleased when I wasn't a virgin, though God knows how he expected me to be. Once the poor darling realised, he wanted to know the ins and outs of every boyfriend before him. And do you know what was even more pathetic? I thought his insane jealousy was evidence of the extent of his love for me. I thought he was crazy about me, and that he'd never look at another woman. I was so stupid. So abysmally, stupidly stupid!'

She began to pace the living room, taking swigs of the whisky as she did so. 'But I didn't stay stupid,' she threw over at Rico, who decided he'd best stay where he was. 'Post-Roberto, I knew *exactly* what men wanted from me and what they felt when they looked at me. Not love, Rico. *Never* love,' she sneered. 'Till Jo came along. I knew *he* really loved me. I knew it wasn't a question of lust with him.'

Rico snorted, his pretend calm finally giving way to his own emotional mayhem. If he was going to lose everything, then he would not go quietly. He'd go down fighting. 'Oh, really?' he scoffed. 'What makes you think that a man of sixty is any different from one of thirty? He *wanted* you all right. And he bought you, lock, stock and barrel. Don't start kidding yourself that all he was interested in was your mind, Renée. That's bull and you know it.'

'For your information, Jo was dying of prostate cancer when I met him,' she countered, stopping Rico in his tracks. 'His treatment had already left him impotent. Sex was *never* a part of our lives together. All he wanted from me was affection and caring and companionship. After Roberto and all the other sleazebags I'd been involved with, that seemed like heaven. OK, so I wasn't madly in love with the man,' she confessed. 'But I liked and respected him. He gave me a lot of happy moments. And he taught me how to give again. He was a nice guy and I won't have you saying he was some kind of dirty old man because he wasn't!'

Rico scooped in then let out a ragged sigh. 'All

right,' he said. 'But it might have been nice if you'd trusted me with that information, Renée. Then I wouldn't have just put my big foot in my mouth again, or had you investigated in the first place. You can't blame me for trying to find out some facts about you. If I waited for you to volunteer things about yourself, I'd wait a bloody eternity!'

At least his forcefully pointing out this truth stopped *her* in her tracks as well. Now her expression was a mixture of confusion and guilt. 'I...I'm not used to confiding in people,' she said defensively.

'Then it's time you learned. And I'm not *people*. I'm Rico, the man who loves you, damn it! The man who's going to marry you.'

Her chin whipped up, her eyes glittering once more. 'You think I could marry a man who had me checked out by a private detective?'

'Yes!' he roared back at her. 'You can and you damned well *will*!'

Her mouth dropped open and she stared, wide-eyed, at him. He glowered back, his knuckles white as they lifted his glass and downed the watery remains of his whisky and melted ice. 'I'm taking no more nonsense from you, Renée Selinsky,' he grated out as he slammed the glass down on a side-table. 'I'm not waiting till the end of the month, either. Tomorrow I'm going out and buying you an engagement ring, and we're going to go over to your place and move those rotten goldfish in here. Then, as soon as we can make the proper arrangements, we will be getting married. That's the new deal and I'm not asking you, I'm telling you!'

Her mouth finally snapped shut and a slow, almost

shy smile tugged at her lovely mouth. 'My, but when you're forceful, Rico, I...I just go to water.'

Rico almost went to water himself at that moment. His bluff had worked. Holy hell!

'Time you saw some sense,' he grumped. 'Now, get yourself over here, woman, and give your fiancé a proper hello kiss.'

She obeyed him, and kissed him, and he wanted to weep. His hands tightened around her and the kiss deepened, his hunger not sexual so much as emotional. He needed to hold on to her and never let her go.

'Rico,' she murmured against his mouth when he lifted his lips briefly for some air.

'Mmm?'

'There's something I have to tell you, too...'

His stomach instantly reverted to panic mode. His head lifted further, his eyes searching hers. 'What now?' he asked tautly.

She looked worried. No doubt about that. She pulled back to arm's length.

'Now, I don't want *you* to be angry with *me*,' she said somewhat hesitantly.

'About what?'

'When I told you about my not being able to have a baby, you—er—seemed to jump to the conclusion that I'd had a hysterectomy.'

'And?'

'My...um...womb is still intact. It's my fallopian tubes that had to be removed. It *is* theoretically possible for me to have a child through IVF, although of course there are no guarantees.'

Rico didn't know whether to kiss her again, or kill

her. Why couldn't she have trusted him with the truth? Why let him think she was totally barren?

But way down deep, he already knew the answers to those questions.

Roberto, again. Rico hoped he'd never meet up with that bastard, or he *would* be guilty of murder.

Still, Renée revealing there was some hope of their having a child together confirmed what he already knew. Renée having his natural baby *wasn't* his first priority in life any more. It would be wonderful. Yes. But it wasn't the only thing. First and foremost was spending his life with this deeply wounded, annoyingly complex but still wonderful woman standing before him.

'Please don't be angry with me,' she whispered, her eyes desperate. 'I…I had to be sure that you really loved me for myself; like you had to be sure that I wasn't a gold-digger. I thought that if after a month of no-strings sex you *still* wanted to marry me then you must truly love me, especially if you thought there was absolutely no chance of a baby. But there was one small hiccup I didn't think of and which cropped up last Monday.'

The penny dropped. 'Your period,' Rico said. 'You got your period.'

'Uh-huh. I didn't want you asking me awkward questions so I did a flit. I can't tell you how awful I've felt, lying to you all week. But I didn't know what else to do. I…I had to be sure of your love. I'm sorry, Rico. Perhaps you shouldn't marry me after all. Perhaps I'm far too screwed up to even think of being any man's wife. Look how terribly I've treated you all these years. Yet all the while I was madly in love with you. I must be some kind of sick sadist. Or masochist. I'm not sure which!'

Rico could not have been more stunned. Or flattered. 'You've loved me all along? You never said so. In fact, I don't think you've said you love me yet even once.'

'See what I mean? I still have difficulty admitting it. Yet I fell in love with you that first day at the races. I thought you were the most handsome, most charming, most exciting man I'd ever met.'

'So why were you so prickly to me? I thought you *hated* me on sight.'

'You had two fateful marks against you. You were Italian, and you were engaged to the type of woman who always brings out the worst in me. I thought...how could he possibly be in love with *her*? And then you looked at me and I knew you weren't. Because I knew that look. I thought...he doesn't love her. He's just marrying her to have babies. He'll be unfaithful. In fact, he'll be unfaithful with me if I let him.'

Rico didn't deny it, because maybe he would have been, if she'd given him an ounce of encouragement. He'd certainly have broken his engagement.

'It was always a battle in my mind,' she went on, 'every time I saw you. God, but I wanted you so much. It was easier to hate you rather than love you. To mock and stir you, *especially* after you got divorced. Your being suddenly available was the most dreadful torment, Rico. I knew I could have you then, but I'd vowed never to get mixed up with another Roberto-type and you seemed awfully similar.'

'I don't see how,' he refuted.

'Think! In my eyes, you were an Italian who married a woman just to have a family, then divorced her once she refused. I couldn't risk giving my heart to another Roberto. I asked you to marry me in that bet because I already knew you had the better hand—you never could bluff me at cards, darling—and I just wanted to see the words. It gave me a secret thrill. I almost wrote ''I love you'' on it as well, just to see *those* words. I never imagined you'd find out. Yet you did! That was awfully clever and very devious of you, Rico. But then, I can see you're a devious man.'

'No, I'm not,' he denied. 'I'm a very straightfor-ward man. I love you and I want to marry you. And I don't want there to be any secrets between us. You're absolutely right, I didn't love Jasmine, but I didn't realise I didn't love her at the time. When you're young, and male, it's difficult to know the dif-ference between lust and love. She also did a damned good job of convincing me that she loved me. We're all susceptible to being loved, Renée. You were with Jo Selinsky. It's a seductive thing, being loved. It was easier to believe that I felt love for Jasmine and only lust for you, rather than the other way around, espe-cially when you were so hostile.'

'I was awful. I admit it.'

He grinned. 'No, you were great. I loved every aw-ful, frustrating moment.'

She looked appalled. 'How could you?'

'I guess I've always liked a challenge. And you were the ultimate challenge. Man, when I got that unbeatable poker hand and you agreed to that bet, I was on cloud nine.'

'I was pretty excited myself. Because I knew what you were going to ask for. By the time we reached that honeymoon suite, I was in such a state. I knew you only had to touch me and I'd come. When I saw that statue, I kept thinking of how you would look without clothes on, and how you'd feel, deep inside me.'

Rico sucked in sharply as his body reacted to her evocative words.

'I couldn't wait to see how you'd look without clothes on myself,' he said, and reached out to start flicking open the buttons on her shirt. 'It's been four days since I've had the privilege and I think I need reminding.'

She didn't say a word till his fingers stopped on the last button. 'What's wrong?' she asked somewhat breathlessly. 'Why are you stopping?'

'Tell me you love me. I want to hear you say the words.'

'That's blackmail!'

'Yep. So speak up, honey, or I'm going to leave any lovemaking till after tonight's poker game. And trust me, I'll do it. Making you suffer comes high on my list of pleasures.'

She pulled a face at him. 'I always knew you were a sick sadist as well. That's why we clicked. OK...here goes. I...love...you.'

'Again, please. And put a bit more feeling into it.'

'I...*love*...you,' she said, and fluttered her eyelashes up at him. 'Good enough?'

He smiled. 'Better.'

'Fine. Now get on with it, will you? We have to be at Ali's suite by eight and it's already after seven.'

'Tch, tch, such impatience.'

'Rico...'

He laughed, and got on with it.

CHAPTER FIFTEEN

SPRING had finally arrived, with Teresa's gardens never looking better. The wisteria was in full bloom over the back pergola and her prized azaleas were having a wonderful season with masses of pink, red and white blooms.

Australian friends had told Teresa not to plant azaleas in Sydney's west. Too hot and dry. But she knew exactly where to plant them—underneath the native trees on the gentle slope which surrounded the large back terrace. She always kept them well fed and watered, and everyone who visited the Mandrettis in spring admired them profusely.

'I've never seen azaleas like those, Teresa,' Renée had said on seeing them. 'I've never had any luck with azaleas myself. Even in pots.'

It was the first Sunday in October, with the traditional family get-together having been swiftly converted into an engagement party. Teresa had only had a week to prepare since Rico had informed her of his news, and she'd worked her fingers to the bone to make sure that everything was perfect for him. The food. The wine. The setting. Nothing was too good for her Rico, and his lovely bride-to-be.

The rest of the family had helped, of course, with the women promising to bring plates of freshly made salads and desserts today, and the men coming the day before to do the lawns and set up some trestles under the terrace. Frederico was still not allowed to do heavy work.

Over sixty guests were expected, most of them direct family. The happy couple had arrived first, as requested, with Enrico immediately taking his father off to discuss where he wanted the kennels and runs built for the greyhounds Enrico was determined to buy his father for Christmas. Frederico pretended to still be reluctant in this venture but Teresa knew he was secretly happy with the idea.

Once the men were out of the way, Teresa had poured herself and Renée a glass of *vino* and they were sitting on the outdoor seating under the pergola, relaxing together.

'People say I have the green fingers,' Teresa remarked.

'And they'd be right,' Renée agreed warmly.

Teresa smiled. 'Speaking of fingers, let me see your ring again.'

When Renée lifted her left hand and wiggled her fingers, the sunlight hit the central diamond, sending out starbursts of colour.

'*Magnifico!*' Teresa exclaimed.

Renée laughed. 'I know. It *is magnifico*, isn't it? Just like my Rico,' she added in a voice that betrayed more to his mother than she ever had to the man himself.

Teresa finally understood why her son had chosen to marry a woman who might never give him a child of his own. She'd been very shocked when he'd first told her about Renée's fertility problem. Shocked and worried. But also proud that her son could love so selflessly. Still, she'd always known that her *bambino* had more love in his little finger than most men did in their whole bodies. She'd been reassured when Enrico told her that they aimed to adopt a couple of children as well as try to have their own. Also, that they weren't going to wait with bated breath for that to happen. Plans were already underway for them to fly to the Philippines and visit several orphanages. Teresa thought that was an excellent idea. Parents who adopted often then had *bambinos* of their own.

'I…I hope you're not too disappointed, Teresa,' Renée added, sensing something in the other woman's silence. 'I know you would have liked a younger wife for your son. One who would pop out babies like clockwork.'

Teresa reached over the narrow trestle table and patted Renée's arm. 'All I want is for my son to be happy. And you make him happy, Renée. No mother could ask for more.'

Renée's eyes flooded. 'Thank you, Teresa. That makes me feel better. Oh, dear, I can hear a car coming up your driveway and I've just made my mascara run.'

'Come…It won't take you long and you will be looking your beautiful self again.'

Which was true. By the time their first guests rang the front doorbell, Renée's make-up was repaired and she was smiling again.

Teresa thought her future daughter-in-law looked even more beautiful than ever, dressed in a feminine and flowing green dress that matched her eyes and showed off her dramatically pale skin and jet-black hair, worn up that day with soft, feathery bits around her face.

But it wasn't Renée's outer beauty that quickly captivated the Mandretti family during the next few hours. It was her genuine warmth, her ease of conversation, plus her obvious love for their favourite son. They'd all lived through Enrico's relationship with that awful Jasmine, and were so happy to see him with a woman of substance and style.

Of course, Rico's own beaming happiness was very catchy. Now that he'd found true love, his natural exuberance for life was overflowing, sweeping everyone along in its rush of sheer joy. Even his best friend, Charles, who could be a serious type of man, could be heard laughing and joking a lot.

The lunch had been devoured and all the adults were sitting around, sipping some of Frederico's excellent homemade wine and feeling very mellow indeed, when a group of the older children came running round from where they'd been playing soccer in the huge front yard. The older girls were inside, talking boys and make-up, and all the younger children had been put to bed for a nap.

'There's this huge truck coming up the driveway, Poppa!' they told Frederico in chorus. Frederico gave his wife a questioning look but she just shrugged.

'Everyone who was coming has arrived,' Teresa told him.

'Let's go see,' Frederico replied and they all traipsed around the side of the house to see whose truck it was.

Rico suspected what was behind the mysterious arrival the moment he saw Ali's royal insignia on the side of what was a large livestock-transporter. He gave Renée a squeeze and said, 'I might be mistaken but I think you're just about to get a new heart's desire.'

She glanced up at him. 'A horse? From Ali?'

'I presume so.' Ali had declined to come to the party, as he declined all such invitations. He said the security measures he had to employ spoilt things for the other guests.

The truck came to a halt not far from the expectant crowd and the fellow driving it jumped out, along with his sidekick in the passenger seat. Both men wore big hats and big smiles.

'Got a horse here for a newly engaged couple named Enrico and Renée!' the driver said, grinning from ear to ear.

'That's us,' Renée said excitedly.

'Nice to meet you, ma'am, sir,' he said, tipping his hat at them. 'Congratulations on your engagement. His Highness, Prince Ali of Dubar, has sent you both a little present, namely one not so little horse. Here's his pedigree and papers.'

Renée gasped when she saw the horse's breeding. 'Rico, look, he's a two-year-old half-brother to Ebony Fire. The same dam but a different sire.'

'That's right, ma'am,' the sidekick informed her. 'And he's a flyer. The boss was gonna keep him himself, he was so fast in the paddock. You are one lucky couple, I can tell you. He's all broken in and been goin' through his paces a treat up home. Just needs some racin' polish. His stable name is Bobbie but his racin' name is Streak of Lightning.'

'Oh, I love that!' Renée exclaimed. 'Oh, I can't wait to see him. Can I see him right now?'

Rico loved seeing her so excited, and so happy.

'No trouble, ma'am. We've been told to get him out and parade him for you for as long as you like, then take him on to Ward Jackman's stables at Randwick.'

The colt was dark grey with a black mane and tail, and highly spirited. Either that, or he was grateful to get out of prison for a while. He reared up on his hind legs a couple of times and danced around, showing off shamelessly for his crowd of admirers. Clearly, the sidekick was an experienced groom because he handled the horse expertly.

'He will get a lighter grey as he gets older,' the groom informed them.

'I have to give Ali credit for his skill as a breeder,' Rico said after the horse had finally been reloaded and was on the way to its new home. 'That is one fabulous horse. And one fabulous gift. I must give him a call and tell him how thrilled we both are.'

He did, straight away, just catching Ali before he left the hotel to fly home. Renée spoke to him as well, thanking him and promising not to beat him at poker for at least a month.

Ali laughed. 'I am too smart a man to fall for that little bluff, Renée. I will now approach next Friday night with even more caution than usual.'

'I had no idea Ali could be so thoughtful, or generous,' Renée remarked on their drive home later that evening. 'He always comes over as rather cold.'

'Ali's not at all cold,' Rico replied. 'He's just another one of the once-bitten, twice-shy brigade.'

Renée shot him a sceptical look. 'I can't imagine the Ali I've seen eyeing up the ladies at the races ever being described as shy.'

'Perhaps shy is not the right word. Wary would fit the scenario better. Wary of opening up his heart, and his emotions. Ali was badly hurt once.'

'By a woman?'

'By a woman, and a man, and his whole family, I would guess.'

'You know a lot about him that I don't know, don't you?'

'Not a lot. Only a little. And only recently.'

'Are you going to tell me the full story?'

'Only if you promise never to tell another soul. Ali would not be happy for this to get around.'

'I promise.'

'I'll tell you after we get home. After we get into bed.'

Renée laughed. 'You have a one-track mind, Rico Mandretti. And that track always leads to the one place. Bed.'

'Actually, I have three tracks. Food, poker and sex. It's just that lately sex has taken precedence over the other two, for which you only have yourself to blame, madam. If you weren't so desirable, I wouldn't spend so much time quenching that desire.'

'I'm not really complaining,' she said, smiling.

'Mmm. Yes, I noticed that.'

'I love you, Rico Mandretti.'

He looked over at her and grinned. 'Well said, my darling. But that was only number seven. Remember, your quota for each day is ten.'

Renée laughed. 'When am I going to be let off that ridiculous quota?'

'When you get the hang of expressing your feelings for me properly.'

'I thought I did that every night.'

'Not in words. I like to hear the words.'

She laughed. 'OK. I love you. I love you. I love you. How's that?'

'Mmm. Not bad. But I think perhaps actions speak louder than words, after all.' And he put his foot down on the accelerator.

The world's bestselling romance series.

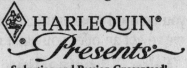

HARLEQUIN®
Presents~

Seduction and Passion Guaranteed!

Legally wed, great together in bed,
but he's never said…"I love you."

They're…

Wedlocked!

The series
in which
marriages are
made in haste…
and love
comes later…

Don't miss

THE TOKEN WIFE by Sara Craven,
#2369 on sale January 2004

Coming soon

THE CONSTANTIN MARRIAGE by Lindsay Armstrong,
#2384 on sale March 2004

Pick up a Harlequin Presents® novel and you will
enter a world of spine-tingling passion and
provocative, tantalizing romance!

Available wherever Harlequin books are sold.

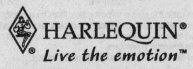

HARLEQUIN®
Live the emotion™

Visit us at www.eHarlequin.com

HPWEDJF

The world's bestselling romance series.

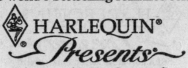

HARLEQUIN®
Presents

Seduction and Passion Guaranteed!

INTERNATIONAL DOCTORS

They're guaranteed to raise your pulse!

Meet the most eligible medical men of the world, in a new series of stories, by popular authors, that will make your heart race!

Whether they're saving lives or dealing with desire, our doctors have got bedside manners that send temperatures soaring....

Coming in Harlequin Presents in 2003:

Pick up a Harlequin Presents® novel and you will enter a world of spine-tingling passion and provocative, tantalizing romance!

Available wherever Harlequin books are sold.

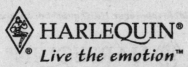

HARLEQUIN®
Live the emotion™

Visit us at www.eHarlequin.com

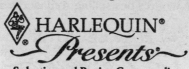

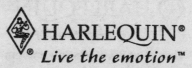

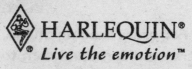